BENDING
WILLOW

JACCI TURNER

A Lucky Bat Book

Bending Willow
Copyright 2013 Jacci Turner
Cover Design: Tatiana Villa

ISBN: 978-1-939051-20-2

LuckyBatBooks.com
10 9 8 7 6 5 4 3 2 1

To my beautiful mother, LaDonna Terry. Mom, you still light up a room and my heart with your smile. I am so glad to have you. I hope you enjoy your farm and the part about Old Blue!

And to Carl Sanford who has been the best thing to happen to our family in a very long time. You are a kind, interesting, and generous man. We love you, Carl!

Acknowledgements

Thank you to Judith Harlan and Cindie Geddes from Lucky Bat Books. They have been with me through it all. Thanks to Louisa Swann, my fantastic editor. She had her work cut out for her, helping me transition from writing young adult fiction to middle grade fiction. She did a wonderful job and I couldn't have done it without her.

Thank you to Tatiana Villa who has made me four beautiful covers! Thank you to Christie Mumm of JLM Creative Photography for my new author pic and to Cindie Geddes for the Burning Man background image on my cover. Dreamstime.com is my go-to site for pictures.

I couldn't do this without my friends in the High Sierra Writers group. My "finished" critique group members shepherded me along the way. Thanks to: Ken Beaton, Jay Leavitt, Patti Doty, Forrest and Lucy Lorz, and Carol Purroy.

This is my first foray into middle grade fiction and I needed a lot of beta readers to keep me on the right track. Thanks to: Jill, Riley, and Mia Tolles; Annette Lane; Michaela Ports; Betty Trujillo; Michelle Brown; and Bethany Spanier.

To Riley and Mia Tolles—Thanks for letting me use your names! I hope you like the book.

I've never been to Burning Man so I asked some 'Burners' for help. Thanks to Sarah Monahan and Cindie Geddes for their input. Any mistakes are mine alone.

As always I am very grateful for my family who gives me unconditional love and support: David, Sarah, and Micah. I love you!

Thanks to God who carries us through difficult times and brings us safely home.

DEAR READER,

I hope you enjoy reading about Riley and Mia's journey as much as I enjoyed writing about it. They have been through some tough times and I'm sure you have, too. I hope you take courage from their adventure.

My husband and I have a lot of people who call us Mom and Dad. They are not ours by birth, but came to us as young adults and have a place in our hearts and in our home forever. I hope you find a place in the heart of an adult, even if it's not the adult who brought you into this world. There is someone out there who would love to share your story. I know I would.

I'm planning to bring Riley and Mia back in another book or two. If you have any questions for me or any ideas for Riley and Mia, please write me at jacci@jacciturner.com.

Gratefully yours,

Jacci

CHAPTER ONE

RILEY BAKER KNEW GRANDMA was dead because she was smiling. Grandma never smiled. Just to be sure Riley pushed open Grandma's bedroom door, crept up to the bed, and watched Grandma's chest...nothing.

She should feel sad about Grandma being dead, shouldn't she?

Riley squeezed her eyes tight to see if there might be a tear waiting to come out, but there was no tear. She felt nothing. Then she heard Grandma's raspy voice in her head, *You nasty, mean, selfish, ungrateful little girl!*

Riley jumped back from the bed, her heart pounding in her ears. Her grandmother lay still—unblinking, smiling. Dead.

Riley shuddered and scooted out of Grandma's room as fast as she could. She went to her thinking chair in the kitchen.

Mornings were Riley's time to think. After Grandma left for work, she'd slip out of bed and curl up on her favorite vinyl kitchen chair, enjoying two full hours of freedom before she had to get Mia up and ready for school. It was the only time of the day she could truly be alone with her thoughts.

But this morning the quiet had shaken Riley awake. Something had been wrong. There was no hacking cough and no deep inhale from Grandma's first morning cigarette. There was no rasp of Grandma's portable oxygen tank. No tink, tink, tink as she stirred her instant coffee into the thermos, getting ready to catch her six a.m. bus for work.

Grandma was a lot of things but late for work was not one of them.

Riley was glad her little sister Mia would be asleep for a while. Mia could sleep through a fire. A fire drill, anyway. They'd stayed in a shelter before they came to live with Grandma. Riley had actually had to pull Mia out of bed and across the floor during one of their shelter's drills. Mia slept through the whole thing.

Once Mia woke up, though, she was a ball of energy that never stopped moving and couldn't stay quiet for one minute.

Riley sat in her thinking spot trying to decide what to do. On one hand, she was scared. On the other hand, this could be a chance for them to escape. Escape from her horrible Grandma and this depressing apartment. Maybe it was even a chance to find her father.

She knew one thing for sure: she couldn't let anyone know Grandma had died. When Mama and Nikko died two years ago, the social worker had taken Riley and Mia to stay at a children's shelter. They'd put Mia in with the little kids while Riley had to stay with the older kids in a different wing of the shelter. Mia cried every night and when Riley overheard one of the staff talking about it, she sneaked into Mia's bed each night after lights out. A good thing, too, because that's where she was when the fire alarm went off. Nobody was taking Mia from her ever again.

Riley took a deep breath. Mia would be up soon. Time to stop thinking and put her plan into action.

Riley took the garbage to the curb so their eighty-year-old neighbor, Mrs. Rodriquez, wouldn't think they'd forgotten to do it and come to remind them. Then Riley packed their school backpacks with carefully chosen items: two changes of clothes each, one extra pair of shoes each, tooth brushes, tooth paste and one hairbrush. She made them each two peanut butter and jelly sandwiches, filled two water bottles, and dumped Grandma's Lemon Head candies into a plastic bag to take with them.

Riley didn't really like Lemon Heads and neither did Mia, but Grandma always kept a jar filled with the sour candy because she said sucking on them helped her cough.

Today was shopping day which meant supplies were low. Riley gave the cupboards one last inspection and was happy to find an open box of what Grandma called her "breakfast of choice," Pop Tarts, jammed behind the instant coffee. There were three Pop Tarts left.

The hardest part was choosing only one book to bring along. The backpacks were too full for more. Riley knew it was wrong to take a library book with her but she just couldn't leave it behind. She'd just started *A Wrinkle in Time* and loved the character Meg. She just *had* to know how the story turned out. She stuffed the book into her backpack before she could change her mind, then put in *Amelia Bedelia*, Mia's favorite.

Then Riley remembered Grandma's change jar. She slid through the door to Grandma's room again, afraid she'd find Grandma sitting up scowling at her, but nothing had changed. The room smelled funny, like when Mia was little and used to wet the bed. Riley started to open Grandma's window and stopped. The bad smell might bring someone looking.

She reached under the bed and pulled out the change jar, feeling like a thief in a candy store. It was an old instant coffee jar filled about halfway with change. The change belonged to her and Mia now, so she wasn't really stealing, was she?

Riley didn't have time to count it all, so she carried the jar to the kitchen and dumped the change into a Ziploc bag. It was all the money they had.

Time to wake Mia. This was where Riley's careful planning could go very wrong. She had to get Mia out the door by nine o'clock as usual so they wouldn't raise suspicion, but she doubted Mia would go quietly once she heard about Grandma. Not that Mia was overly fond of Grandma. But, Grandma had been less mean to Mia than to Riley, and you just never knew about Mia. When Social Services had finally tracked down their grandma, it was obvious she hadn't wanted the girls. It was the small check from the state each month that changed Grandma's mind—plus Mia's ability to charm a rock.

"Here goes nothing," Riley whispered as she sat on the pullout next to Mia. She began to hum their wake-up song, the one their mother had sung to them every morning before the car wreck changed their lives forever. Mia twitched and Riley began to sing the song about welcoming the sun. Mia's eyes popped open and she smiled her gap-toothed smile. *Somehow she always wakes up happy,* Riley marveled.

Mia threw her arms around Riley in a morning hug, then rolled out of bed to help straighten the blankets and fold the bed back into the couch. They'd been following this routine every morning for a year now and Mia never complained. She was born with Mama's sunny temperament, Riley thought as she did every morning. Mia and Riley had the same mom, but different dads. Probably good that Mama had kept their last names different. Mia Mongelli definitely fit Mia better than Mia Baker. Riley wrinkled her nose, trying to imagine herself as Riley Mongelli and failing. Am I more like my dad? she wondered.

Whenever Riley missed their mother, she just had to look at Mia to see her. Mia had Mama's long golden hair, the kind of hair that billowed wildly no matter how hard Riley tried to tame it. She had Mama's huge hazel eyes, too. Eyes that danced when she smiled, which was most of the time.

Riley was the exact opposite of Mia in every way—tall and thin with stringy dishwater-colored hair and a long face. Her worst feature, in her opinion, was her forehead. It was extra high. Mia could swing from happy to stormy in two seconds flat, just like Mama, whereas Riley was steady as a rock and just as quiet. When Mia was unhappy it was like all the sun had been taken from the sky and locked away. When Mia was happy, the world was a much better place.

Riley filled Mia's cereal bowl with what was left of the cereal, poured her the last of the milk, then took her usual spot across from Mia at the green

Formica table. She pulled strips off her dry heel of toast and chewed slowly, not sure how to begin.

"Mia," she started. Mia looked up, chewing with her mouth open. Riley normally corrected Mia's manners, but she ignored them this time. "Mia, something happened last night."

"What?" Mia asked, her eyes growing impossibly larger.

"Well, you see...Grandma died." Riley hadn't meant to just say it like that, but now it was out. She held her breath.

"No, she didn't!" Mia said, smiling as if Riley was teasing.

"Actually, she did, Mia...and that means we need to leave."

Mia jumped out of her chair, ran down the short hall and through Grandma's bedroom door before Riley could stop her. Riley chased after her. "Mia, stop! You don't want to..."

But Mia was already up on Grandma's bed, her hands on each side of Grandma's head, staring into her smiling face. Mia stayed like that for a full minute, the longest Riley had ever seen her be silent. Then Mia jumped off the bed and ran back to the table. When Riley got to the kitchen, Mia was shoveling cereal into her mouth again.

"You're right," she said around her cereal, bits of corn flake and milk flying.

Riley studied Mia's face for a storm of tears and saw nothing, not even a cloud.

"O-kay," Riley began gingerly. "Now that Grandma is dead we can't stay here and we can't tell anyone about Grandma."

"Why not?"

"Remember the shelter?" Riley asked, bracing herself. The shelter was a subject they both avoided talking about.

"You mean we have to go back there?" Riley could see the fear and a small glisten of a tear begin to well up in Mia's eyes.

"No, no." Riley moved to Mia's side and put both hands on her sister's face, trying to coax back the tears before they turned into a midsummer thunderstorm. "No, listen. We don't *have* to go back there." Riley tried her hardest to sound excited like she was about to tell Mia they were going to the circus or sneaking into one of the side gates at the rodeo before all the people arrived. "We can leave today before anyone finds out."

"Oh," Mia said, searching Riley's face. "Okay."

Riley relaxed as Mia went back to her next scoopful of cereal.

CHAPTER TWO

A T EIGHT FIFTY-FIVE they were ready to go. Mia had been asking non-stop questions that Riley brushed off with, "I'll tell you on the way."

Riley took one last look around the apartment and spotted Grandma's purse hanging next to the door. She grabbed the purse, took it to the kitchen table, and dumped out the contents. In the midst of wadded-up Kleenex, Riley found an open pack of gum plus seven dollars and some change in Grandma's wallet. She also found a bus pass and the keys to the apartment. Attached to the keychain by a clip was a small black tube. Grandma showed it to her once, explaining in her gruff voice, "It's mace. Anyone tries to mess with me—I spray 'em in the eyes and say, 'Take that sucker!'"

Riley unclipped the mace canister from the key ring and put it in the front pouch of her backpack.

"Take that sucker!" Mia sounded like a tiny Grandma. The girls exchanged a smile.

They slipped on their backpacks as they stepped outside into the August heat. Even though they'd been in Reno for a year, Riley still missed the cooler temperatures of the San Francisco bay. She locked the front door, then took Mia's hand and headed down toward the street. Instead of turning left to go to school, they turned right and began to walk toward the city bus stop.

Mia skipped beside Riley and began to ask her questions. "What's gonna happen to Gramma?"

"Bill will find her tonight," Riley assured her sister. Bill was Grandma's boyfriend. At least that's what the girls called him behind her back. Grandma just called him Bill or sometimes Grumpy. Every Monday night Grandma went to Bill's place with a new bottle of whiskey to play what Grandma called "grown-up games." Mia thought they probably played Monopoly because it was a hard game and took so long to play. Riley wasn't so sure. All she knew was that Grandma came back late reeking of booze and slurring her words. She always looked like she'd been in a wrestling match with her hair and clothes messed up.

Mia nodded. "Yep, when she doesn't show up with the bottle, he'll come lookin' all right. What about school?"

School had just started last week and Riley liked her new teacher, Mrs. Taylor. She thought sixth grade was going to be her favorite grade yet. It was sad she didn't even have a chance to say goodbye. Mrs. Taylor liked books as much as she did and didn't even think Riley was odd when she chose to sit inside reading instead of going outside for recess.

"I called this morning and told them we had the chicken pox. That way they won't miss us for a while."

"What's the chicken's box?" Mia asked with a high-pitched giggle.

"*Chicken pox* is when you get these spots all over your body and have to stay home for a week. We got them at the shelter, but the school doesn't know that."

"I didn't get no chicken's pox."

"You didn't get *any* chicken pox," corrected Riley.

"That's what I said."

"Actually, I got them first and you only had two or three on your scalp."

Mia rubbed her head. "Where are we going?"

"We're going to Idaho to find my dad."

"But Daddy died in the car accident with Mama."

"Remember how Nikko was your dad but Mama told us I had a different dad?"

"Oh, yeah. I forgot. But how we gonna find him?"

"Well, I asked Mama once where he lived and she said Idaho. I asked 'Where is Idaho?' and she said, 'You just hop on Interstate 80 and head east.' So, I figured we'd try to take a bus heading east 'til we get to Idaho."

"Does he know we're coming?"

Riley was afraid to answer this question. Not only didn't her dad know they were coming, he didn't even know she existed. She reached back and patted her pocket. It contained the envelope with the name Blaine Baker and an address that was her only link to her father. It also held the letter her mother had sent to him telling of her pregnancy with Riley. It had been marked 'return to sender' on the front and was unopened.

Riley didn't want to worry Mia. "Not exactly, but I'm sure he'll be glad to see us."

When they got to the end of the block by the Albertson's supermarket, Riley held Mia's hand so they could cross the street to the bus stop. She hoped there were no truant officers out today.

Mia whined, "I gotta go pee!"

"I told you to go before we left."

"I didn't have to go then."

Riley turned back toward the Albertson's store. She'd taken Mia in there before to use the restroom. Might as well get it over with before they got on the bus.

Inside the store the air was cool and refreshing. Pallets and pallets of water and camping equipment were stacked all around. It looked more crowded than usual. Lots of people in strange outfits and funny hair pushed carts full of water and food. At first Riley was confused, then she remembered it was Burning Man time. Mrs. Taylor had told her class that Burning Man was a big party for artists in the Nevada desert. It brought lots of strange people to town,

Riley held the stall door for Mia inside the dingy bathroom. A clerk in an Albertson's uniform was cleaning the sink while a woman with bright ribbons woven into her hair washed her hands. Riley tried not to stare but the woman was interesting to look at. She had bright green shorts that were so short they looked like they would have fit better on Mia and colorful tattoos running up and down her bare arms. She had a kind face.

The clerk spoke to the lady with the ribbons. "Are you going to The Burning Man?"

Riley had a hard time understanding the clerk's heavy accent but the woman seemed to understand perfectly.

"Yes," the woman said, "I go every year. Are you a Burner?"

"No, I'm new to this country. Where is The Burning Man, anyway?"

"Oh, it's out in the Nevada desert, just east of here on Interstate 80..."

Riley's heart sped up—east on Interstate 80? That's where her mom said they needed to go to find her dad! *I wonder if she'd give us a ride?* If Riley could get them a ride, she'd save money on the bus and they didn't have much money. On the other hand, if she asked for a ride, the woman might ask where her parents were and might call the police or something when she found out they were on their own.

When they left the bathroom, Riley found herself looking for the woman who she now thought of as Ribbons. Sure enough, Ribbons was in the checkout line with a guy pushing two huge carts piled with groceries. Mia was begging for a candy bar, so Riley let her pick one and chose an Almond Joy bar for herself. She went through the self-checkout as she'd seen Grandma do, keeping her eye on Ribbons and the guy. The guy's hair was almost as long as Ribbons' and hung in strange strands that looked like black snakes. He had tattoos on his arms too, but they weren't as pretty as the ones Ribbon had.

Riley lingered around looking at magazines until Ribbons and her guy left the store. Then she grabbed Mia by the hand and followed behind Ribbons until they got to a huge painted bus. Riley could tell it used to be a school bus, but now it was painted all over with the same kind of pictures that were tattooed on Ribbon's arms. Did Ribbons paint the bus herself? If she did, she was a good painter.

The girls stood off to the side, eating their candy bars and watching Ribbons and the guy with the snake hair Riley now thought of as Snake. Ribbons went to the front of the bus and pushed the door open.

"We need your help," she yelled inside. Two guys came off the bus walking slowly, like they'd been woken up from a nap. They looked as odd as Ribbons and Snake. Riley could almost hear her grandma's gravelly voice saying "Hippies!" in disgust. That was the same word her grandma had used to describe Mama and Nikko—hippies. So, these folks must be okay.

Riley remembered what Mama had said about taking rides from strangers, but she also remembered what her mom said about listening to her *uh-oh* voice. "We all have a voice inside that tells us when we are in danger," Mama had said.

Riley had asked, "How do you hear it?"

"Sometimes it feels like butterflies in the pit of your stomach," Mama had told her. "Sometimes like prickles on the back of your neck. Sometimes you just hear an *uh-oh* in your mind..."

Riley stared at the bus and tried to feel her body. No flutters, prickles, or uh-oh's. She had an idea...

Two more women pushed full carts up to the bus. The guys from inside had climbed up on top of the bus near the back. The four down below began to hand the groceries up to them. Riley grabbed Mia's hand and pulled her to the side of the bus as if they were just walking by. When they got to the open door, she whispered in Mia's ear. "Follow me and be quiet."

Riley carefully climbed into the bus followed by a wide-eyed Mia. What if someone else was on the bus? What would they do then? Riley's heart beat in her throat as she frantically looked around. Startled, she realized that where the bus seats had been, couches now sat with boxes stacked in between them. Other than the boxes, the bus was empty. It was warm and stuffy inside, smelling of sweat and fast food.

"Get down," Riley said, crouching below the windows. She looked for a place to hide but the couches were too out in the open and the boxes all seemed to be full.

"Okay, last one. Make sure you strap it tight!" Snake yelled somewhere outside.

Riley grabbed Mia's hand and pulled her quickly to the back of the bus. Boxes were stacked across the back, blocking the view of the rear window. Riley risked a peek over the top box and found herself looking right at Ribbons. Riley jerked back. Had Ribbons seen her?

Her mouth went dry. Why had she come on this bus in the first place? What was she thinking?

Voices began to move from the back of the bus toward the door. She had to think fast. Riley risked another glance over the boxes. She could just see the back of the last girl turning to push the empty carts away. They were coming back onto the bus!

Riley turned to Mia and put her finger to her lips. She picked her sister up and set her over the wheel well into a long, narrow space behind the boxes. Mia barely fit. How was Riley going to squish back there? She heard a foot hit the bus stair. She stepped over the tire well, squeezing herself into the narrow space. For a moment she didn't breathe. She and Mia looked at each other. Mia's hands flew up to her lips, suppressing a giggle. Riley clamped her hand over Mia's mouth.

Leaning down, she whispered, "Mia, we can't make a sound, understand?" Mia nodded gravely.

Suddenly the bus rumbled to life, a noise so loud Riley felt safe taking her hand from Mia's mouth. The stinky smell of the diesel engine filled her nose. People laughed as they entered the bus. Rock music began blasting from speakers, the door squeaked shut, and the bus lurched forward.

Mia and Riley slammed against the back window and the wall of boxes in front of them leaned slightly toward them.

Riley eyed the boxes. *What if they fall and crush us back here?* Riley could tell by Mia's wide eyes that her sister was wondering the same thing. Should they speak up? Tell someone they were here? Beg the people to stop and let them off the bus? But then there was the issue of the shelter. She glanced down at Mia and felt her resolve return. Nope, no one was taking Mia away from her again.

Riley realized that if they turned sideways, she and Mia could sit on the floor facing each other. They settled down on the hard floor and Mia whispered, "Why did we get on this bus?"

Riley leaned toward her. "Because it's going east on Interstate 80."

"Oh. Why are those people dressed so funny?"

"I think they're artists. They're going to Burning Man."

"They're going somewhere to start a fire?"

"I don't think so..."

"I hope they don't start a forest fire," Mia said, eyebrows knit together.

"Burning Man is out on the playa," Riley said firmly. "Mrs. Taylor says there are no trees on the playa, so there can't be a forest fire."

"That's good," Mia said. She opened her pack, pulled out her stuffed bear, Mr. Witherspoon, propped the bear behind her, and promptly fell asleep.

Riley shook her head. How did Mia manage to fall asleep so quickly, and in such strange circumstances, like she didn't have a care in the world? And when did she sneak Mr. Witherspoon into her pack? Riley smiled. Mia had chocolate on her face from her candy bar and her hair splayed out around her head like a giant curly halo of gold. She's my angel, thought Riley, laying her head against the hard bus wall and wishing she'd thought to bring a bear.

CHAPTER THREE

B RAKES SQUEALED and Riley's head hit a stack of boxes, thumping her awake. *Where was she?* Slowly she remembered—Grandma was dead and they were in the back of a bus headed east on Interstate 80. She was surprised to realize she had fallen asleep; maybe it was the heat and the rocking motion. Mia still snoozed against the other side of the bus. Riley listened. The sound of the engine seemed quieter and the bus had slowed considerably. She could even hear some of the conversation.

"Now, you're all virgins," Snake said in a loud voice. "So when we get there, after they inspect the bus, you'll have to go through initiation."

"What's the initiation?" a female voice asked.

Ribbon laughed. "Oh, don't worry. It's nothing; just fun."

"What are they inspecting us for?" a male voice asked.

"Don't worry," Snake replied. "They're just looking for stowaways. People are always trying to sneak in."

Stowaways, thought Riley, that's what we are. What did they do with stowaways? She wanted to ask, but didn't dare. Thankfully, Ribbons answered for her. "The Black Rock authorities are pretty hard on stowaways. They take them back to Gerlach and dump them, and if they try to sneak back in, they arrest them."

Riley sucked in her breath. They could get arrested! What would happen then? Jail would be worse than the shelter. Panic rose in her throat. She glanced at Mia still peacefully sleeping and exhaled. They would have to pass the inspection, that's all there was to it.

What was The Burning Man, really? All Riley knew was that a bunch of artists had some kind of big party in the desert. That didn't sound so bad. But what about the initiation of the virgins? That sounded scary.

She couldn't worry about all this at once. She had to think about what was most important. What was she going to do about the inspection and why were they going so slow? Riley pushed herself up onto her knees. Her bottom tingled from sitting so long on the hard metal floor. She slowly stood, stretching up to her full height. It felt good to stand and she braced herself so she wouldn't knock into the boxes as the bus bumped and jostled along.

She peered out the window, struggling to see. Dust swirled all around them. When the air finally cleared, Riley found herself staring at a long, long line of cars and trucks snaking through the desert behind them. The whole line was headed in the same direction. She couldn't see where they were all going, and didn't dare look around the boxes to try and see out the front. It looked like they were driving on the surface of the moon. There wasn't a tree or plant in sight, though she could make out some mountains in the distance.

What was she going to do about the inspection? They couldn't be found. She looked at the wall of boxes. The box on the bottom was a long rectangle with an opening in one end near Mia's back. It looked like a sleeping bag was stuffed into the open end of the box. Suddenly, Riley had an idea. She shook Mia awake, pressing a finger to her lips to remind Mia to be quiet.

Riley leaned over and pointed. "Mia, see this bottom box?"

Mia rubbed her eyes, looked where Riley was pointing, and nodded.

Riley whispered, "When we get where we're going, there will be an inspection. We need somewhere to hide. Can you pull that sleeping bag out of there?"

Mia got onto her knees and pulled at the sleeping bag. It came out easily.

"What else is in there?" whispered Riley.

Mia leaned her head into the box and looked. She sat up and shrugged. "I can't see."

"Can you get more out?"

Mia reached into the box and pulled more things out—blankets, a camping stove, dishes. Soon she had to crawl further and further into the box, backing out to hand what she found to Riley. Riley quietly stacked the belongings behind her until there was so little room in their space she was practically standing on top of Mia.

Mia crawled out and stood next to Riley, reaching up to whisper in her ear. "That's all."

"Okay, Mia. This is what we're going to do. You crawl into the box feet first. Then I'll crawl in feet first. We can hide in the box until after the inspection."

"But I've gotta go pee," Mia said.

"You're gonna have to hold it," Riley said sternly.

"But I'm hungry."

"Okay, we'll eat something before we go in." Riley opened her backpack and gave them each one peanut butter and jelly sandwich. The music blasting from the front of the bus turned to a new song and the Burners started loudly singing along. Riley knew this song; it was one of Nikko's favorites. He sang with his thick Italian accent which made the girls giggle. He always played this song on their road trips, making them all sing at the top of their lungs.

Mia smiled up at Riley. They munched their sandwiches, heads bobbing, and quietly joined the singing. The next song was unfamiliar. The girls drank some of their water and then crawled into the box. It was dark and stuffy inside.

"I can't breathe," Mia mumbled.

"We just have to stay in here until after the inspection," Riley said.

"But I can't breathe!" Mia said, her voice growing louder.

"Shh!" Riley sighed. "Okay, let's switch places."

Slowly, they crawled out of the box. Riley lifted Mia around her.

"Okay," Riley said. "We'll wait till we're sure they are stopped before we get back in. I'll go first this time."

She was glad they waited. It took another half hour for the bus to get up to the inspection station. Suddenly, the door opened and someone outside shouted, "Welcome Home!"

Quickly, Riley crawled feet first into the box. Mia was right. It was hard to breathe in there and really hot. It didn't help that her nose was next to Mia's dirty feet. But her head was closer to the opening than Mia's had been and she would just have to make do.

"Mia," Riley's whisper echoed off the sides of the box.

"Yeah?"

"Pull something in front of that hole."

Mia was quiet for a minute. "I'll put my back-pack there." The box suddenly went pitch black.

"Great idea," Riley said. "You can't fall asleep, Mia. All right?"

"All right."

"Promise?"

"I said all right, didn't I," Mia said. Riley could hear the irritation in her sister's voice. Better be careful. They couldn't afford to have Mia start storming in this box.

"Great. I trust you. Thanks," she said and hoped Mia was right.

CHAPTER FOUR

R ILEY COULD FEEL Mia's body tighten as the
inspector walked closer to the back of the bus.
She snaked a hand up to give Mia's ankle a comforting squeeze. She could clearly hear his voice as he
leaned around the boxes. A tiny bit of light flashed
into their box. Did he have a flashlight? What if he
mentioned the pile of stuff they had taken out of
the long box and stacked up? What if Ribbons or
one of the others looked back and found their stuff
all messed up before she and Mia got off the bus—
would they tell the inspector?

"Looks good," the inspector said. "I'll take your
tickets now. Next stop is the Greeter Station, then
you're into the city. Welcome home!"

The bus riders responded with loud whoops
and hollers as the doors closed and the bus moved
forward. Riley blew out a breath she didn't realize
she'd been holding.

"Okay," she whispered. "We'd better get out quietly now."

When she and Mia had climbed out of the box, Mia's face was bright red and damp hair clung to her face. Riley took a deep breath. Even diesel fumes smelled better than Mia's feet! Riley wiped sweat from her eyes, shoved a water bottle at Mia, and chugged a long drink. They had to figure out a way to get off the bus without being seen. She didn't know what the initiation of the virgins was, but she didn't want any part of it. Should they sneak out during the initiation or during the unpacking?

The bus stopped again and the door opened. A happy voice said, "Welcome to the playa. Any virgins aboard?" A cheer went up in the bus. "Well, step outside and give me a dusty hug!"

The bus bounced up and down every time someone got off. After the sixth bounce Riley whispered to Mia. "We have to get out so I can see what's happening."

Mia started handing back the things she'd pulled from the box. Riley contemplated putting everything back into the box but that would probably take too long. She started a pile right behind her, stacking one thing after another as fast as Mia handed them to her. Finally, there was enough space to climb out.

"Climb over, Mia, then get down low," Riley whispered. "Don't go any further until I check and see if it's safe to get off the bus. I'm right behind you."

Riley and Mia clambered over the boxes and crawled up to a window. Riley peeked out and saw rows of cars with dusty people hugging the new arrivals. Ribbon and her friends were clustered together with their backs to the bus. Did Ribbon's group knew those dusty people? Otherwise, why would they be hugging?

"Now!" Riley grabbed Mia's hand and dragged her forward. If they left now, they could probably get off the bus unnoticed. Her heart raced as she pulled Mia out the door and abruptly turned away from the crowd. Desert heat hit them like a blast from a furnace.

We made it! Riley sighed.

Suddenly, someone grabbed her from behind. She twisted in the tight grip and saw Mia being lifted into the air. "Virgins!" yelled her attacker.

Riley felt like she'd been punched in the belly as she watched Mia carried away on a lady's shoulder. Riley kicked backwards with all her might and connected with her captor's leg.

"Ow!" shouted a male voice and she was promptly let go. "Dang, kid. I wasn't going to hurt you."

Riley bolted into the crowd, following Mia's bobbing head. The lady carrying Mia suddenly plopped her down onto the dusty ground and began rolling her in the dirt. Stunned, Riley watched as Mia giggled. More hands came out of nowhere, pushing Riley to the ground and rolling her around in the dust. She glanced up at all the smiling dirty faces and didn't try to fight. A large hammer-like object was thrust into Riley's hand.

"Come on, girls. Hit the gong!" the woman who'd carried Mia said.

Riley got up and walked toward the large flat gong. She hit the metal softly with the hammer. The gong gave a small "tink" and fell silent.

"It's okay," the woman said. "Give it a smack!"

Riley hit the gong harder and a loud resonate sound echoed around them. Then Mia took the hammer and swung it with all her might and the crowd cheered in delight. Riley eyed the crowd of happy faces. Everyone seemed to be in a happy mood. Many had braids and ribbons in their hair. Some wore clothes that reminded Riley of Halloween outfits. Behind the crowd, Riley saw Ribbons and her group climbing back into the bus. She felt a little sad to see Ribbons go, she had liked her.

Now Riley had to figure out how to get to Idaho from wherever they were.

A crowd of people who looked like they'd recently been rolled in the dirt moved toward a town. Riley grabbed Mia's hand and followed. She did not want to stand out and risk getting caught. Weird that there was a town in the middle of nowhere like this. As they moved further from the cars and into the town she saw it wasn't a normal town at all. People were camping in the streets. Riley felt like she'd landed in a circus. People were dressed in strange costumes—some had hats and feathers and colorful scarves. Many had tattoos and decorations in their hair like Ribbon. Several wore very little. Mia pointed as one old man, wearing nothing but a hat, rode by on a bicycle.

"He's naked!" Mia said in a voice loud enough to wake Grandma.

Riley pushed her sister's arm down. "Don't point!"

They stood, staring like watchers at a parade as more oddly-dressed people went by. Most wore goggles and scarves around their necks. Many rode bicycles and some drove cars that were as decorated as they were. What exactly was this place and why did everyone look so strange?

More importantly—how they were going to get to Idaho?

Riley heard Grandma's gravelly voice in her head, *You stupid, stupid kid. What have you done now?*

"I have to pee," Mia said.

Riley looked around. Tents and other structures formed the border of the town, but she didn't see anything that looked like a bathroom.

A woman wearing a gauzy blue outfit walked by, her outfit flowing around her in the breeze. She was playing a game with some long sticks, using two sticks to throw a third into the air. She smiled at the girls as she walked by.

"Excuse me," asked Riley. The woman stopped. "Can you tell me where a bathroom would be?"

"Over there at eight o'clock," the woman said, pointing to their left and forward with her long stick.

"Are they only open at eight?" asked Riley, confused.

"No," the women said and came over to the girls. "Look," she said, pointing into the distance. "The town is set up like a clock. The man is at twelve o'clock and we are standing at six. The port-a-potties are at eight."

"Oh...thanks," Riley said, still confused. The lady smiled, began playing with her sticks again, and walked off.

Riley grabbed Mia's hand and started walking, still not sure which way to go. The wind helped cool their skin, but it was also blowing fine dust onto their ankles, covering their flip-flops and lower legs.

A man rode by on a bike pulling an empty trailer covered in fur.

"Mister," shouted Riley. He stopped the bike and turned to her. Riley took a step forward. "Can you tell us where the bathrooms are?"

"Hop on," he waved and the girls climbed onto the trailer. He peddled hard across the dusty playa and

Riley was amazed at how big the place was. Finally he stopped and pointed at a long line of port-a-potties.

Riley jumped off and pulled Mia after her. "Thanks!"

The man tipped his cap and rode away.

Riley looked at the long rows of pink and blue port-a-potties. This place would be easy to remember. "Mia, if we ever get separated from each other, let's meet here. Okay?"

"Okay," agreed Mia. "I'm thirsty."

"Let's go potty first. Then we can find some shade and have a drink."

SHADE WAS NOT as easy to come by as Riley first thought. The girls walked and walked until she spotted a tall wooden man in the distance. Is that what the lady had been pointing at? The tall man? If he was the top of the clock, then they were about ten o'clock on the imaginary map the lady with the sticks had described. There didn't seem to be any shade except in the camps that lined the border of the town. Riley looked at Mia's red face. Her little shoulders were starting to burn. They had to find somewhere to rest out of the sun.

Taking a deep breath, Riley approached a camp that had a huge shaded area. Several people were resting on couches and chairs in the shade. Riley approached a man who looked like Santa Claus sitting in a fold-out chair. Anybody who looked like Santa had to be nice, even if he was only wearing flowered shorts.

"Can we sit in your shade?" Riley asked nervously.

"Of course!" Santa boomed. "Shade is free here, like everything else!" He laughed heartily.

"Thanks," Riley said, pulling a wide-eyed Mia away before she could say anything.

"Was that Santa Claus?" Mia asked as Riley led her further into the camp's shade.

"I don't know. Maybe this is where he spends the summer." Riley found two camp chairs and sat down, grateful to be out of the sun. She pulled out their water bottles and both girls drank deeply. Mia turned around in her chair, staring at Santa. The smell of cooking bacon made Riley's stomach growl. Mia's stomach growled at the same time. Riley thought about what the man had said, "Shade's free...like everything else." What had he meant? Was food free here, too?

"Who's hungry? We got breakfast for dinner," came a high-pitched voice behind them. Riley turned to see a huge woman cooking in what looked like a kitchen near the back of the shade structure.

"I am," answered two people lying together on a couch.

"I am," Santa shouted.

"I am," Mia yelled, popping up from her chair.

"Shh." Riley tried to pull Mia back.

"But I'm hungry," Mia insisted.

"Then come and eat, sweeties," the huge woman said with a kind smile.

Mia ran over and Riley hesitantly followed. "Are you sure it's okay?" Riley asked as the woman handed her a plate of bacon and eggs.

"Fine by me if it's okay with your folks." The woman's high voice did not match her large body.

"My folks are dead," Mia blurted.

Riley's eyes flew open. "But we're here with our uncle and he won't mind," she stammered.

Mia turned to Riley as if to correct her. When her little mouth opened, Riley popped a piece of bacon into it. Mia began to chew.

"Say 'thank you,' Mia."

"Thank you!" Mia mumbled around the bacon.

"Thank you very much," Riley added and turned, guiding Mia back toward their chairs.

Riley leaned toward Mia and whispered as they ate. "If people find out we're here without our folks, they might tell the police. If someone asks, we tell them we're here with our uncle, okay?"

"But we don't have an uncle."

"Okay, but let's pretend we do."

"Then I get to pick his name."

"Okay, Mia. What is our pretend uncle's name?" Riley asked, exasperated.

"Umm...Uncle Meriwether!"

"Can't he have a normal name like Uncle John or something?"

"Nope. You said I could pick and I picked Uncle Meriwether."

"Okay," Riley agreed, feeling exhausted. How on earth was she going to keep Mia out of trouble and how would they ever get to Idaho?

CHAPTER FIVE

"YOU TWO WANT TO help me with the dishes?" asked the woman who had served them dinner.

"Sure," Mia said, happily jumping up. Riley followed behind her.

It felt good to put her hands in the sudsy water and help scrub the dishes. Mia was drying, handing the dishes back to the woman.

"My name's Peggy Sue," she said. "What are your names?"

"My name's Mia," Mia said with enthusiasm. "This is my sister Riley. Is that man over there Santa Claus?" Mia pointed at the shirtless man snoring in his chair.

Peggy Sue laughed. "Well, he's not the real Santa. Might be one of his helpers though. We call him Bad Santa."

This made Mia squeal with laughter. "Bad Santa," she repeated. "Bad Santa. Bad, bad, bad!"

Then Mia launched into a list of questions. Riley groaned.

"Did you get rolled in the dirt?" Mia asked. "Did you bang the gong?"

Peggy Sue laughed again, "Oh, you're virgins, are you? Nope, I've been coming to Burning Man for years. Been a long time since I got rolled."

"When are they going to burn the tall man?" Mia asked, her eyes wide.

"They burn at the end of the week," said Peggy Sue.

"Really?" Mia asked, eyes even wider. "But why do they do that? He's so big and beautiful."

Peggy Sue chuckled, "Well, it's why we come. We live here for a week to...get away from the hustle and bustle of our lives...to live as one big family. Everything here is temporary. All the art...it either has to be burned or taken home with us."

"I wish I could take the big man home with me," Mia said. Riley watched Peggy Sue's eyes dance. Mia had charmed her way into Peggy Sue's heart, just as she did with everyone. Not for the first time Riley envied Mia's easy way with people.

Peggy Sue bent down and looked at Mia's red shoulders.

"Oh, honey. You need some sunscreen." Peggy Sue poked through the boxes behind her until she found a tube of sunscreen and started rubbing it on Mia's shoulders, arms, and face. Then she handed the tube to Riley who carefully rubbed the cream on her own arms and shoulders.

"You keep that; I have more," Peggy Sue said. "Did your uncle bring you goggles and scarves for your faces? You'll need those when the wind comes up. It can be brutal."

Mia looked at Riley, uncertain. Riley shrugged. "I don't know what he packed. Is there somewhere we can buy them if he didn't?"

"Oh, you can't buy anything at Burning Man. It's a gift economy."

"What's a gift e-non-nome?" Mia asked.

"Oh, we all 'gift' things to each other. It's part of being a community. You were hungry so I fed you, and you helped me by doing the dishes. You see how it works?"

Riley nodded. She remembered how her step-dad, Nikko, used to trade working on people's cars for things like getting their toilets unclogged. He called it a barter system which sounded similar to a gift economy. "So is there someone here we could trade something with to get goggles or scarves?"

"Oh, I don't know about that," Peggy Sue said. "It's not a trade economy. It's a gift economy. People give things away without expecting anything in return." She rummaged around in the boxes some more, finally pulling out blue cloths. "Here, take these for now. They would fit around your faces in an emergency."

"Thanks," Riley said, examining the strange cloth.

"What are they?" asked Mia, trying to tie the cloth around her face.

Peggy Sue took the cloth, folded it into a triangle, and tied it around Mia's face so she looked like a bank robber. "They're just disposable towels. It's the best I can do." She pulled the towel down from Mia's nose so the fabric rested around her chin. "You can wear it like that, then if the wind comes up, pull it over your noses and close your eyes. You can duck into some cover until the wind stops." Riley tied her scarf and then pulled it down around her neck like Mia's.

"Well, we'd better get back to our uncle's now," Riley said. "Thank you very much for everything!"

Mia threw her arms around Peggy Sue. She giggled when her arms didn't make it even halfway around. "Wow, you're big!" Mia said.

Riley's face burned with embarrassment. Why did Mia have to say everything that came into her mind?

Mia hung on tight. "I like hugging you. You feel like my teddy bear, Mr. Witherspoon!"

Peggy Sue laughed. "Oh, Mia. I'll miss you. Come by and say 'Hi' from time to time, will you? And if you're hungry, and I'm here, you can always eat with us."

"Thank you, Peggy Sue." Mia's words were muffled by the woman's stomach.

"Come on, Mia. Time to go," Riley said, pulling Mia away. They waved and smiled at the woman one more time, then stepped out into the sun.

The air felt cooler than when they had first gotten off the bus. The sun was lower in the sky and the temperature was dropping. Riley and Mia walked as if drawn by an invisible cord toward the center of the town. The closer they got, the more crowded it became. The place looked more and more like a carnival than a town. One man, walking by on stilts, threw beaded bracelets down to them. Someone else was handing out chocolate chip cookies. Riley wished they'd brought something to share. Then she remembered the Lemon Heads packed in a plastic bag in her bag. She dug the bag from her backpack and opened it.

"Mia, if you want, we can share these." Riley held up the bag.

"Okay," Mia said. She grabbed the bag from Riley's hand and raced from person to person offering everyone a candy.

Not exactly what I had in mind, Riley thought, but she enjoyed the delighted faces of the people when Mia held up the bag. Mia offered a Lemon Head to a boy who was about Riley's age. Riley's heart dropped when she realized he was the first kid she had seen. Burning Man was full of grown-ups! How were they going to blend in if everyone here was old? Then she relaxed—Peggy Sue didn't seem to think it was odd for them to be wandering around.

"Riley, look who I found!" Mia said, dragging the bewildered boy up to her as if he were a long-lost relative.

"Hi." The boy, who stood a head taller than Riley, grinned a crooked smile that looked more like a smirk. "I'm River."

Heat rose in Riley's cheeks. She was not used to talking to boys outside of school—or inside of school for that matter.

"I'm Riley," she mumbled.

"Riley, eh? Zat your Burning Man name or your regular name?" he asked.

"My regular name, I guess..."

"You're virgins, aren't you?" asked River, briefly lifting a sailor hat off his head like some kind of weird salute. His hair was spiky blonde with red tips. Riley's face got hotter. She bit her lip; maybe he'd think she was sunburned.

Thankfully, Mia interrupted. "Yep, we got rolled in the dirt just this morning and got to ring the gong. Now can I have a Burning Man name?"

River shook his head, "You can't just pick a Burning Man name. You have to wait 'til the name finds you. I didn't get a new name until my second trip to Black Rock City. That's what this place is called, ya know. I been here three times now. My uncle brings in a big installation from California and my dad brings an art car from Utah. I'll take you if you wanna see it."

"What's an install-lation?" Mia asked.

"It's one of the big art pieces. Burning Man's about radical self-expression. It's the hot place for artists. I'll show you." He turned and Mia took his hand. Riley followed behind them.

Riley wasn't sure she liked this boy. He seemed full of himself, throwing around big words. He probably just wanted to look like a know-it-all. At least he was dressed, which was more than she could say for many of the people here. He was wearing shorts and a t-shirt with a leather-fringed vest over it and that funny sailor hat. He had goggles and a kerchief around his neck like everybody else.

They passed an area with thousands of Barbie dolls lining the entrance. Barbies were everywhere inside as well. Riley and Mia gawked as River led them around the outside.

"Just turn left at the Barbie Death Village," River said, "and my camping space is one block back."

Riley hadn't realized the town went back from the center in blocks.

River continued, "Most of the camps have themes, like the Barble Death Village. We don't have a theme, but we bring one of the best art cars."

They passed camp after camp until they finally arrived at a small camp with tables set under blue tarps strung between white pipes. Beyond the covered area a huge dragon was being unloaded from the flat bed of a large truck.

"Look, Riley, look," Mia shouted, bouncing on the balls of her feet and pointing to the dragon.

"What is it?" asked Riley.

"It's an art car," River said as if that were the most obvious answer. "You can't bring any vehicle into Black Rock City unless it's an art car. Ours just happens to be one of the biggest. Once it's unloaded I'll ask my dad to take us for a ride if you want."

"Yes, yes, yes!" Mia jumped up and down, her face glowing.

Riley wasn't sure she wanted Mia on top of that giant monster, but River did seem to know a lot about Burning Man. Maybe he'd know how far they were from Idaho, too. River stepped into a small motor home parked next to the shade structure. He came out with a handful of beef jerky which he offered them.

Well, Riley thought. At least we won't be starving here.

They stood there, chewing beef jerky and watching as a team of people unloaded the dragon, easing it down a ramp.

River ran over to a tall thin man in a wide-brimmed hat and sunglasses. Riley could see River gesture their way. He was grinning broadly and bouncing on his toes. To Riley he looked like a regular kid, instead of a bossy know-it-all. Then he waved for them to join him. He led them around to the back of the dragon and up small set of stairs. They found seats on the benches that lined the dragon's back. The benches were set so low only Riley's head and shoulders were above the dragon's back. River waved at the people helping. "This is Dad's crew. They'll take turns driving the dragon this week, but we all pile on for the inaugural ride of the season."

The dragon was a beautiful purple color, his neck and head stretched out far beyond the front of the truck. His four legs spread out over the tires so he seemed to be gliding over the desert, his long tail following after them.

Riley started to relax and enjoy the ride. This was the best way to see the town...*Black Rock City*, she corrected herself. As the art car made its way around the city, she could see why they'd been told the place was laid out like a clock with the tall man at twelve o'clock and the camps spreading out in a circle from there. From their perch on the dragon's back, they were able to see miles of what River called "art installations" they never would have seen on foot. The installations were amazing, some as tall as a building—like the giant metal letters spelling out Love—or the beautiful metal sculpture of a naked dancer towering above the people below her. Riley watched as one girl mimicked the statue's pose and another took pictures. There was a rocket that people could climb up into and lots of different kinds of dragons. One dragon shot out of the ground like a sea monster emerging from the sea.

River acted as tour guide. "That's Thunder Dome," he said, pointing at a large dome-shaped cage on their right. "You can go in there and fight. It's fun. You can be hooked to a bungee cord and climb up the walls."

"Did you fight?" Mia asked. She was standing up on the bench so she could see, steadied by Riley's hands.

"No, Dad won't let me yet. He said I have to be sixteen. But that's only two more years. I can't wait."

He pointed at a place that looked like a large fountain. "You can take a shower there but I don't. I spend the whole week good and dirty."

Riley's nose wrinkled at the thought of this boy after a week of not washing.

River grinned and raised a dust-covered arm. "The playa dust keeps the bacteria down. That way you don't smell. The dust helps keep you from getting sunburned, too."

Riley looked down at her dusty feet and legs. They had been in the sun all day without sunscreen and felt fine, unlike her shoulders. Maybe River was right, but she hated the thought of not showering for a whole week. Not Mia though. Mia's smile covered her whole face.

The sun was almost down and it was really beginning to feel cold. Riley took Mia off the bench, pulled some warmer clothes out of her backpack, and helped her little sister dress. They layered pants and sweatshirts over their shorts and tank tops. Riley hated putting socks on over the playa dust, but couldn't see any way around it. When she looked up again, the city had turned into a magical world of lights. Lights were everywhere. The dragon even had lights lining its sides. They rode under a huge arch that barely missed the top of the dragon's head. "Second Biggest Little City" was spelled out in brightly-lit letters across the arch.

Mia gasped and pointed as people on stilts lit the tall lamps that circled the city all the way out to the giant wooden man.

"The theme this year is fertility," River continued as they rumbled on. "All the art installations have

to be connected to that theme in some way. Hey—
see this area at ten o'clock?"

River pointed at an area with lots of people talking and laughing loudly. Riley nodded.

"Stay away from there," River said with a serious expression.

"Why?" asked Mia.

"Trust me. That area is for...grownups."

Mia and Riley looked at each other and nodded,
saying in unison, "Grown-up games."

"Right," River said, his eyebrows rising. "Tomorrow I'll take you out to see my uncle's installation."

Tomorrow, Riley repeated silently. She tried to
push the worry down in her stomach. *I guess we
won't be getting to Idaho tonight.*

CHAPTER SIX

THE NEXT MORNING Riley woke as a beam of sun came through the tarp above her and hit her straight in the eyes. It took her a minute to remember where she was. She sat up, looking out. The camps all around them were quiet.

After leaving River, she and Mia had found a camp that was big and mostly deserted. The city really came alive at night, like downtown Reno on a weekend, but the folks in this camp must have been somewhere else. There was a couch with a blanket draped over it. She and Mia had snuggled under the blanket, so if anyone came back and saw them asleep, they would just think it was one of the other camp members.

Riley rubbed her face, grimacing at the dust on her hands. Had they really ridden a dragon last night? What a wonderful, weird end to a crazy day. She was already starting to feel at home here.

They were supposed to meet River at the Barbie Death Village around ten. He had a watch; she didn't. She would just have to ask someone although with the little people wore, a watch might be hard to find. She let Mia sleep a little longer, then began her wake-up song. Mia smiled and greeted Riley with a dusty hug. No matter what Mia did during the day, Riley couldn't help but love her in the mornings.

After finding the port-a-potties they went in search of food. "You do the talking," Riley said to her sister. "People always like you."

Mia nodded. It was probably too soon to go back to Peggy Sue's place without someone asking questions, so they wandered from camp to camp. Most people seemed to still be sleeping. Finally, they found their way to the Barbie camp. There were people sitting around a table drinking coffee. Mia walked up to the table while Riley stood back.

"Hi, I like your dolls," Mia said.

"Cool," said a man with a patch of fuzz growing on his chin.

Mia rocked from foot to foot while everyone at the table stared at her. Finally she said, "Do you have any food?"

"Where are your parents, little girl?" asked a woman with rings through her eyebrow, her nose, and her lip.

Riley held her breath, not knowing what Mia would say.

"Still asleep," Mia said.

Whew, Riley thought. That's my girl!

The man with the straggly beard got up and rummaged through a box. "Here," he said, handing Mia an apple.

"Thanks," Mia said, standing there for another minute before walking back to Riley.

"Well, you tried," Riley said. Mia stuck out her lower lip. Maybe breakfast wasn't going to be the easiest meal to find here. Everyone looked tired and cranky like Grandma did after her night of "adult games" with Bill.

"Hey," Riley said. "We still have food in our bags. I was saving it but there's lots of food here. Let's save the apple and eat our second sandwiches now."

Mia smiled and they found a spot in a different camp to sit and eat. Riley shook her water bottle—almost empty. She would have to remember to ask River where they could get more water. Even though River could be annoying, he was handy to have around.

After breakfast they played in the dirt near the Barbie camp, drawing hopscotch boards with their fingers and using small rocks for markers. Mia saw River first and ran to greet him. When they got back to Riley, River handed them each a pair of swim goggles.

Mia put her goggles on. "River's gonna take us to his uncle's stall-ation."

Riley filed in behind as River and Mia moved ahead. River gave Mia a playful shove as they walked and she shoved him right back. Why did everyone like Mia so quickly? Riley felt invisible and kicked a rock as Mia and River laughed. River could be such a jerk with his know-it-all attitude, then do something nice like hand them goggles, then turn around and act like she didn't even exist.

They caught a ride on a chain of golf carts decorated to look like a caterpillar. The carts took them out to the tall wooden man. Up close the wooden statue was huge. River pointed to a large building in the distance. "My uncle helped with the Temple this year. The Temple is the biggest burnable structure on the playa, even bigger than the Man. The Temple burns each year but not until after the Man burns. In my opinion, the Temple is cooler than the Man because it's more meaningful."

Riley glowered at River's back. If he thought using big words would impress her, he was wrong.

They had to catch another ride on an art car to get to the Temple. Riley forgot her anger as they got closer. The building was huge and beautiful with a domed roof and several floors she could see people walking on. Inside was even better because it was cool and smelled of cut wood. There were art pieces and beautiful wood carvings of plants and trees. As she looked closer, Riley could see handwriting on the walls of the temple.

"What's this?" she asked River.

River ran his hand over the markings on the walls. "People write things here, like the names of friends who have died or things they want to forget. Then when the Temple burns, they let it all go with the flames." He raised his hands, wiggling his fingers.

Riley was fascinated by the walls. She walked around, reading all the different inscriptions. She felt sad reading the names of people she didn't know who had died and things like "my broken marriage," "my dog Jake," "my cancer."

Mia and River were going up the stairs to a different level.

"Coming?" asked River.

"One minute," Riley said.

She picked up one of the many markers placed around the inside of the Temple in wooden containers. She wrote on a beam, "Mom, Nikko, Grandma." That was all she could think of for now.

Out of all the things she'd seen so far at Burning Man, the Temple was her favorite. There was something quiet and beautiful and...something else. She didn't have the words for what it was, but somehow being in the Temple reminded her of Mama.

CHAPTER SEVEN

B Y THE THIRD DAY, Riley was pretty tired of Burning Man. She was sick of the heat and the dust and she wanted to get back on their trip to Idaho, but she hadn't figured out how to do that yet. She was also tired of watching grown-ups act like kids, drinking at night and being grumpy in the mornings.

They followed River around for a part of each day, Mia bugging him for a Burning Man name and River saying it hadn't come yet. They learned to stay up later and sleep in longer so they could find breakfast in the morning. They also learned to brush their teeth in the port-a-potties because you weren't allowed to even spit toothpaste into the playa dust. Because of this, Riley only made them brush once a day, another bit of happiness for Mia.

They found shade and took naps in the afternoons. Their favorite place was the Cat-in-the-Hat structure in the Dr. Seuss camp. It was a nice place to sit and had green eggs in the morning. Most of the camps were willing to fill their water bottles. Riley was surprised that no one questioned their stories about having an uncle somewhere in camp.

They ended up sleeping on the same couch each night. The camp was called Playa International and most of the people staying there were from other countries. They were very friendly, treating Mia and Riley like members of the camp. Riley met people from places she probably couldn't even find on a map. Two Israeli girls spent hours braiding Mia's hair into little braids all over her head and weaving in colorful ribbons. They would have done Riley's hair too but she turned them down. They did talk her into adding a few ribbons though.

On their fifth day in camp, the first sandstorm hit. It was still morning and Mia had found a few kids to play with who were closer to her age. They were kicking a ball around while Riley sat watching them play. She tried to read her book but her mind kept wandering.

How were they going to get to Idaho?

She'd come to the conclusion that she was going to have to ask River for help. Just thinking about asking made her stomach do flip-flops, but she could think of no other way. She was considering how to ask when she felt the wind blowing dust into her eyes. Riley bolted to her feet. She couldn't see Mia or the other kids anymore. Dust swirled all around, so thick she could barely see two feet in front of her. She pulled on her swim goggles. The goggles helped keep dust out of her eyes, but they didn't help her see.

"Mia, Mia!" Riley ran toward where she had last seen the children, choking on the dust that flew down her throat and into her nose. She remembered her kerchief and quickly pulled it up over her nose and mouth.

Would Mia remember her kerchief?

"Mia!" Riley screamed again, panic rising in her throat.

"Quick, come in here," a woman yelled. Someone grabbed Riley by the arm and dragged her into a tent. The flap closed suddenly and she heard a zipping noise. Riley swallowed a scream, struggling to reach the tent door, but somebody held her back.

"Let me go!" Mia was out there somewhere in the dust.

"You can't go out in that dust storm. You need to stay here until it passes."

Riley yanked off her goggles and spun toward the sweet voice. She stared up at the beautiful blonde woman who'd been holding her, a woman with blue eyes, a freckled nose, and hair pulled back in braids.

"But Mia is out there," Riley said. "My sister is out there."

"Don't worry," the woman said. "Someone will take care of her until this passes."

Riley looked around the tent room. It was huge, much bigger than most tents. The floor was covered knee deep in pillows. "Where are we?" she asked, confused.

"This is my favorite place to come and rest and get out of the weather," the woman said. "It's put here for that purpose. I came to give Juliet a nap." She waved at a pile of pillows near the back wall where a toddler was sleeping.

"A baby?" She hadn't seen a baby in Black Rock City until now.

"Yes," said the woman. "I'm Poppet, and that is Juliet."

Riley looked at the closed tent flap. "Are you sure my sister will be okay?"

"I'm sure, and I'll help you look for her after the wind dies down if you want."

Riley felt guilty about not insisting that she had to look for Mia, but she loved that tent, she loved Poppet, and she loved Juliet most of all. Poppet was with the Playa International group and had only come for the last two days of Burning Man. "Burning Man can be hard with a baby," Poppet said, nodding at the sleeping child.

Riley could see why. Juliet was at that age when babies were into everything. After she woke up, she ran and stacked pillows and climbed them and never stopped moving. Suddenly, Riley realized she could stop feeling responsible and just relax. She wasn't too hot, she wasn't too cold, and she didn't have to keep an eye on Mia, although she did still worry about her.

Poppet was wonderful. She talked to Riley as if she were an adult, asking her opinions about music, movies, and life in general. Riley knew she'd never have an older sister, but if she did, she'd want her to be just like Poppet.

The wind howled for two hours, but for Riley, it was over too soon. She was playing patty-cake with Juliet when the tent flap unzipped. A huge man entered the tent and instantly pulled Poppet into a hug.

"I hoped I'd find you here," he said. "The worst of it's over now." Juliet ran and flung herself against the giant's knees.

Poppet turned toward Riley. "This is Thunder Cat, my husband."

Wow! Thunder Cat was possibly the tallest man Riley had ever seen. He was wearing what looked like a brown skirt and huge black work boots with a flowing red cape tied around his neck. His head almost hit the top of the tent, but he seemed incredibly gentle as he held both Juliet and Poppet in his arms.

"Hey, Scout," he said to Riley with a friendly smile. "Haven't I seen you around the camp?"

"Yes," Riley said. "My sister Mia and I...Mia!" She dashed for the open tent flap. Then she ran back and gave Poppet a hug, reaching up to squeeze Juliet's chubby arm. "Thank you so much," Riley said.

"Do you want me to help you look?" Poppet asked.

"No." Riley ducked through the flap. "I think I know where she'll be."

Riley stood outside trying to orient herself. The lamps of center camp and the port-a-potties weren't that far away. Would Mia remember their meeting place?

It only took a few minutes to reach the port-a-potties. Riley raced up and down the rows, shouting Mia's name. Her voice got hoarse as the minutes ticked by. Finally she heard the most beautiful sound in the world.

"Riley!"

Riley spun around as Mia pulled away from the woman who'd been holding her hand and dashed into Riley's arms. The woman waved and turned away.

"I was so scared in the wind," Mia said in Riley's ear. "But Tabitha's mom came and took us into her tent and then brought me to find you."

Poppet had been right, Mia was fine.

CHAPTER EIGHT

R ILEY KNEW IT WAS NOW or never to ask River for help. She'd been putting it off, not knowing what to say, but time was running out. He'd taken them out into what was called the "deep playa" so he could show them what the playa looked like when no one walked on it. A bright orange plastic fence glistened in the distance. River explained the boundary was fenced because if you left the city and got lost, you could easily die in the desert.

Riley stared down at the flat, cracked ground outside the camp. The white dirt lay in patches that looked like Grandma's scaly dry skin. If you walked on it, it felt hard under your feet like a road. The dirt in camp was all churned up and dusty, but this dirt looked like something prehistoric. Riley half-expected a dinosaur to come running up at any moment.

"Can we go to your camp for lunch for a change?" River asked.

This wasn't the first time he'd made that request. Riley had always come up with an excuse as to why they couldn't go back to their camp. Today her answer was different. "River, we need to talk."

He glanced up.

"You see," Riley continued before she lost her nerve. "Mia and I aren't really here with our uncle." She waited to see how he'd react to this news.

"Okay..." River looked at Mia, then back at Riley. "Then who you here with?"

"Well...we aren't really here with anyone," Riley said. "We came as stowaways."

"What?" asked River. "You snuck in? Do you know how hard that is to pull off?"

"We hid in a box," Mia added.

River shook his head, "You're saying you've been here all week with no parents or uncles or anything?"

"That's right," Riley said. Would River be mad and turn them in?

A crooked grin spread over River's face. "Wow, that's amazing. You're way more awesome than I thought!"

Riley wasn't sure whether to feel complimented or insulted.

"So why did you sneak into Burning Man?" River asked.

The girls rushed to tell the whole story, stepping on each other's words in their excitement. They told about Grandma and trying to find Riley's father and needing to get to Idaho.

River shook his head. "This definitely calls for Burning Man names," he said when they'd finished. He stood and placed a hand on Mia's head. "Mia, I hereby christen you...Sparkles!"

Mia laughed and danced around. Sparkles was perfect for Mia, but what would he call Riley? What if it was something she hated?

"And you, Miss Riley..." River looked at her thoughtfully for a long time before placing a hand on her head. "I hereby christen you...Willow!"

"Willow," she repeated. "Why Willow?"

"Ah." River smiled his crooked grin. "Willows are strong and flexible and graceful and..." He looked down, kicking the ground with his shoe. "Beautiful," he added, looking shyly into her eyes.

Heat flooded Riley's cheeks. *Graceful, strong, flexible, and beautiful.* Did he really see her that way?

River clapped his hands together, making both Riley and Mia jump. "First, we need to figure out exactly where you're going. Let's go back to camp and look at the map Dad keeps in the truck. Then... well, we'll take this one step at a time." He marched off toward his camp, taking Mia's hand and leaving Riley to catch up — as always.

IN THE CAB OF THE BIGGEST pickup truck Riley had ever seen, River opened the map and studied it for a long time. Riley and Mia were in the back seat with River in the front. She peered over his shoulder, suddenly dismayed. They weren't close to Idaho at all!

River pointed at a place on the map. "Here's where I live, in Utah. Now that's a lot closer to Idaho than we are now." He pointed to a large white spot on the map. "We can get you a ride going east, but you'd have to get another ride from right... here." He stabbed the paper with his finger. Riley squinted at a town called Wells. "To get to where you're going you need to head north from Wells."

"Do you think your dad could take us to Wells?" Riley asked.

"Wait." River said, flicking his hand as if she were a fly. "I'm thinking here."

Riley clamped her mouth shut, scowling. She'd like to tell him what he could do with his old map but they needed the help. She'd never met anybody who could make her feel happy, then mad, then happy so many times in one day.

"I can't think in here," River said, folding up the map and putting it back in the glove compartment. He jumped down from the truck and slammed the door, then paced back and forth in front of the bumper.

Riley and Mia looked at each other and shrugged.

Riley was just about ready to give up when River yanked open the passenger door. "I've got it! Follow me," he said and marched off.

They walked past three small camp sites before River stopped, turning to them. "You let me do all the talking," he said, pointing his finger at each of them. "Got it?"

Riley gritted her teeth and nodded.

River leaned down and tapped on the zipper of a small tent with the words *U.S. Army* stamped on the side. "Hubcap? Hubcap, it's me, River."

A minute ticked by and then the tent zipper opened from the bottom up.

A tangled mass of hair poked out of the tent. Riley was sure there was a man in that mass somewhere but she couldn't see him. A hand came up, sweeping most of the hair back, revealing an old bearded face with unfocused eyes. A gravelly voice from somewhere in the beard said, "What's up, little brother?"

River waved at Riley and Mia. "These are my friends, Willow and Sparkles. They're from Wells. Their mom had to go back to work and I told her we could drop them off at the Flying J on our way through town. Can they ride with you?"

"No problemo, little brother."

"Thanks, Hubcap. I'll bring them over tomorrow after we're packed."

"No worries. Now, if you'll pardon me, I will resume my siesta," Hubcap replied, pulling his wild head back into the tent.

Riley stared at River. "You did it!" she whispered as they walked away. She'd worried about this problem all week and he'd solved it in ten minutes.

"Told you I would," River said. "I have to help Dad pack up now 'cause we leave early. I'll meet you at the Temple when the sun goes down. You guys better pack up too."

Riley tugged her backpack straps. "All packed," she said.

River walked away, shaking his head.

THE TEMPLE BURN was completely different than the burning of the wooden man. *That* burning had been a giant loud party and the fire that consumed the Man was huge. Most people packed up and headed home the morning after the Man burned, leaving the city quieter and more peaceful.

The crowd of people gathered for the Temple burn sat silently on the ground in front of the three-story structure. Riley wished she could run her hands over the wooden scrollwork covering the front of the building one more time. She loved the intricate cutouts of animals framing the large doors. She would be sad to see this building burn. The silence reminded Riley of the time her mother and Nikko had taken her to church for Mia's christening. The hush of the crowd and quiet expectation made her insides tremble.

She sat between Mia and River, not the usual order of things, but River had plopped down next to her when he'd arrived. It was pitch black outside. Mia's hand snaked into hers as she stretched up to whisper in Riley's ear. "I wrote Mama, Daddy, and Grandma's name in there. River helped me."

Riley smiled. She leaned down and kissed the top of Mia's head. "I did too," Riley whispered. The girls pressed close together.

Suddenly, the crowd grew so silent Riley wondered if everyone had stopped breathing, and then there was fire: beautiful, terrible, consuming fire. All the pain of thousands and thousands of people burned before their very eyes. Riley felt tears on her cheeks and turned to see them on Mia's face too. She looked at River, who smiled and slipped an arm around her shoulders. Riley felt her heart squeeze with hope as she watched the flames. Maybe she *would* find her father after all.

CHAPTER NINE

RIDING WITH HUBCAP turned out to be an adventure in itself. Riley spent most her time wondering if the old beat-up Dodge, stuffed with dirty camping gear, would make it all the way to Wells. Wire held the car's hood down as they bumped down the road and the duct tape on the seats scratched her bare legs. She and Hubcap sat in the front with Mia between them, her sweaty legs sticking to Mia's whenever they touched. Riley finally gave up expecting the car to fall apart every time they hit a bump and spent the rest of her time wondering what they would do when they actually got to Wells.

Mia listened with wide eyes as Hubcap told story after story of crazy adventures from his life. It seemed his stories got a bit more ridiculous every time he heard Mia giggle. At least his stories kept Mia busy. Riley watched the sagebrush slip by. Maybe when they got to Wells, they could find a bus heading north. Except for buying the candy bars on the way to Burning Man, she'd spent none of the money she had brought.

When they finally reached Wells, Riley realized that catching a bus might not work. Black Rock City had been a much bigger city than Wells. In fact, Wells seemed more like a wide place in the road than a city. They pulled into a Flying J gas station and it was one of the few buildings Riley could even see. Hubcap drove up to the gas pump and Riley saw the dragon car along with a bunch of cars and jeeps belonging to the other camp members pull in behind them.

The girls got out of the car and stood next to Hubcap, baking in the heat as he filled the tank of the dusty Dodge. Riley looked at the other vehicles in their caravan—all were covered in white playa dust. So were the people climbing out of the cars. Mia and Hubcap were covered too. That meant she must be covered. Riley chewed her lip. How were they going to clean up? They couldn't ask anyone for a ride looking like desert rats.

Someone touched her shoulder and Riley jumped. She turned to find River looking down at her. He was as dusty as the rest but his crooked smile seemed to light up his face. He glanced at Hubcap.

"I'm going to walk the girls in and make sure they find their mom," River said.

Hubcap gave both of the girls a dusty hug and they followed River into the store. The building was much bigger than Riley had thought and the air conditioning felt amazing. There were rows of things for sale from food to clothing to movies. A clock on the wall told Riley it was 2 p.m. Mia started to head for a lunch counter at the far end, but River pulled the girls toward back of the store, down the hall by the bathrooms where they wouldn't be seen.

He glanced around, then pulled a folded paper from his pocket, and handed it to Riley. "My Face-book name, in case you want to keep in touch."

Riley took the paper and slowly unfolded it. Two words were scribbled in red ink: Lukez Sil-vashy. "Lukez?" she asked.

"Yep, that's my real name."

"Oh." She smiled shyly up at him. "I like it."

"You two ought to stay in the bathroom 'til we're all gone. I'll tell Hubcap your mom was here and took you out the back door." River stood, shift-ing from one foot to the other, then leaned down and placed an awkward kiss on her cheek. His face was red as he said, "You take care now. Let me know when you get where you're going."

Riley nodded. She reached up carefully and touched her burning cheek as River knelt down and gave Mia a huge squeeze. "You take care of each other for me, will ya?"

The girls nodded. River stood and walked away. Then he glanced back over his shoulder. "And come back to Burning Man next year so we can hang out again, okay?"

Riley smiled and waved. Probably not, she thought. Then again, if someone had told her a week ago she'd be running away and having all these crazy experiences, she never would have believed it. *Miracles happen. Maybe I will see you again, River.* She desperately hoped so.

RILEY FROWNED as she and Mia stared at each other in the bathroom mirror. How would they ever get clean enough to ask someone for a ride?

"Number 35, your shower is ready."

The announcement bursting out of the loud speakers startled Riley. Then she grinned. "Did you hear that, Mia? We're going to take a shower!"

Mia frowned.

When Riley felt they'd been in the bathroom long enough for everyone to leave, she grabbed Mia's hand and headed down the hall. A quick glance into the main store showed the coast was clear. She dragged Mia up to the check-out counter, promising her lunch if she'd just keep quiet for a minute. The clerk, a teenage girl with a large nose, looked down at them and her lip curled like they were a couple of ugly bugs "Can I help you?"

"My mom asked me to buy us a shower," Riley said with as much confidence as she could muster.

"Burners cost more cause they take more water," the clerk said as if Riley was about to use the last drop of water in Wells, Nevada.

"Okay."

"Seven bucks. You're number 42."

Riley gulped and carefully counted all the bills in her hand. Exactly seven. But they *had* to have that shower. If they didn't get rid of this playa dust, they'd never be able to get a ride. She handed the money to the clerk with the attitude and received a small receipt with the number 42 on it.

"I'm hungry." Mia groaned and held onto her stomach like she was starving. "You promised!"

"Let's look around first," Riley said. They needed food, but it had to be something that didn't cost too much. She wandered down one aisle after the other, shaking her head as Mia pointed out cookies and chips. Riley found a small travel-sized shampoo and decided they'd use shampoo as soap for their shower.

Then Mia spotted the pizza. "You promised!"

She dragged Riley over to the glass display case and pointed. The pizza smelled delicious. They could get one huge piece and a coke for five dollars. Riley carefully counted out five dollars in change from her bag of Grandma's coins. The bag was still mostly full but it was largely dimes, nickels and pennies. She'd used most of the quarters. There was no way they would be able to afford a bus ticket now.

After eating camp food for a week the pizza was the best thing Riley had ever eaten and the soda was so refreshing she thought she might die of happiness. She slowly chewed the last bite as the loud speaker squawked again.

"Number 42, your shower is ready."

"That's us, Mia. Come on."

They headed back to the counter where the cranky clerk jabbed her finger toward a hallway as if Riley was an idiot for asking how to find the showers. Riley led Mia down the hallway past an open room labeled "Truckers Lounge". The room had a big screen TV and several truck drivers lounged around in comfortable chairs watching TV or talking.

Mia gasped. "Look..."

Riley clapped her hand over Mia's mouth, stunned by the sight of their two faces on the TV screen. It took a moment to realize the pictures were last year's school photos. With the dust covering them and the braids in Mia's hair, they didn't look like those pictures at all.

"...the girls have been missing over a week now and authorities still have no leads on their whereabouts. If you have any information, call Secret Witness..."

Riley swallowed hard and glanced at the truck drivers. No one was looking at them. She pulled Mia away from the TV and down to the women's showers. The room was bright with clean white paint, a long mirrored wall, and several shower stalls. Only one had a key on the outside. She bet down to check and saw feet in every other stall. Slowly she opened the door with the key and found it empty. Inside sat a small bench, a clean towel, a bath mat, and a tiny bar of paper-wrapped soap. There were even hooks for hanging clothes on. That's when Riley realized she'd never paid for the shampoo. She had put it in her pocket when the pizza came and forgotten about it.

Forget it, she decided. They'd paid enough for this shower. They shouldn't have to pay for shampoo, too. Still, she couldn't just steal the shampoo. She'd pay for it before they left even if they'd been overcharged for the shower.

Riley looked at Mia's hair. "We're going to have to take out those braids."

"No, I don't want to." Mia backed away, shaking her head.

"I'm sorry, Mia. It's the only way your hair will get clean."

This argument went on until Riley firmly pushed her sister down on the bench and began pulling the rubber bands off the ends of Mia's braids. Mia sat still, tears streaming down her face, as Riley untangled the thin braids. Mia's sulking gave Riley time to think. She was scared and her mouth felt dry.

They were wanted by the police. Did the police think they had killed their grandmother?

No, Riley told herself. It was an Amber alert. She'd learned about them in school. The police thought they'd been kidnapped. Her heart pounded. Should they turn themselves in? Then they might never get to Idaho. She might never get to meet her father. They might be taken to a shelter again.

The week at Burning Man had felt like a vacation from the real world and now the real world was crashing down on them. Once they got this playa dust washed off, they'd be recognizable. What should she do?

CHAPTER TEN

NOTHING HAD EVER FELT better to Riley than that shower. She and Mia used every bit of the shampoo and that tiny bar of soap to get clean. There was plenty of warm water and Riley let Mia stay in the shower even longer than needed. Might as well get their money's worth.

They picked the cleanest shorts and tank tops they could find in their backpacks, then Riley pulled out the sunscreen the big lady had given them their first day at Burning Man. She spread the sunscreen over their arms and faces.

Combing the tangles from Mia's hair in front of the shower room mirrors was another harrowing adventure but Riley promised to put two braids in Mia's hair when all the tangles were gone.

"Three, I want three braids," insisted Mia.

So Riley copied what she'd seen the Israeli girls do with three parts of Mia's hair. She had one braid on each side and one in the back, though Riley thought the one in back looked silly. Mia admired herself in the mirror while Riley combed her own hair out. She decided to put her hair in braids too, thinking it might help them look different than the pictures on the TV.

She was stalling. They were going to have to leave this bathroom sooner or later. She glanced up at the black clock above them, almost four o'clock. It was getting late. Riley took a deep breath, grabbed Mia's hand, and headed out the door.

A trucker leaned against the door frame of the Trucker's Lounge. He was shorter than some of the other truckers Riley had seen and his arms looked too big for his t-shirt. He turned and watched them walk toward him. Riley wasn't sure she liked the way his eyes narrowed, then widened. He smiled. "Hey there, little ladies. Where you headed this fine day?"

"We're going to Idaho," Mia said before Riley could stop her.

Riley pulled Mia forward, but the trucker walked along beside them. "Really? That's where I'm going. Do you need a ride?"

Riley stopped. They did need a ride. And they needed to get away from this place and its TV as soon as they could, but...something felt wrong. Still...

"Actually we do," Riley said before she could talk herself out of it.

"Great!" the trucker said with a big smile. "Follow me. My rig's right outside."

He walked out the side door of the Flying J to ward a large truck with a white cab, the kind of truck Nikko had called an eighteen wheeler. He climbed up on the step to the passenger door, then pulled the door open, glancing around as if he'd forgotten something. Riley's stomach felt a little funny—she'd been taught not to take rides from strangers—but they'd already found rides twice and everything had gone okay.

The trucker held out his hand and Mia grabbed it. He lifted her into the cab of his truck. Riley let him take her under her arms and lift her up, next to Mia. His eyes were green, like a cat's, but his big smile didn't light up his face the way River's smile did. She jumped when he closed the door behind her.

The inside of the truck was huge and smelled like cigarettes and dirty socks. This truck was different than River's. The front seats were separated by cup holders. The girls sat on the passenger seat which was plenty wide for both of them. The truck driver climbed into the driver's seat and started the engine.

"Let me help you with your seat belt," he said, reaching around the girls and pulling the seat belt forward. His scratchy chin brushed Riley's forehead. She smelled his cigarette breath and shivered.

"I'm Todd," he said, raising his voice over the loud engine. "What are your names?"

Riley leaned forward and said quickly, "I'm Willow and this is Sparkles."

"Willow and Sparkles," he repeated, raising his eyebrows. "Those are some interesting names."

"Yep," Mia said. "River gave them to us."

"Hmm," Todd said. He turned the truck toward a sign that said "93 North" and started driving down the highway.

Mia asked question after question about Todd's truck and he seemed happy to answer them, keeping up a steady stream of conversation as he drove. Riley glanced around the cab. There was a space for walking between the seats and a bed behind the seats with what looked like a curtain tucked to one side. As they rolled down the highway the sun got lower in the sky. It seemed like they passed miles of cow pastures without really getting anywhere. Then, just past a town called Jackpot, Todd pointed to a sign on the side of the road. "Lookie there, girls. We're now entering Idaho."

Riley could just make out a sign that read "Welcome to Idaho" in the fading light. Her heart leapt. They were in Idaho! Would she finally meet her dad? Would he want her? Riley's stomach clenched. After all they'd been through what if her dad didn't want her?

Mia's head began to bob and soon she was asleep on Riley's shoulder. Todd reached over and laid his hand on Mia's leg. The light of the dashboard made deep shadows under Todd's eyes. He glanced at her, green eyes glowing. "Poor little tyke's beat! We should probably pull over and catch some shut-eye."

Riley noticed Todd didn't remove his hand from Mia's leg. The butterflies came back into her stomach. What had she been thinking? She didn't know this man!

"I thought we were going into Idaho further," she said, her voice shaking.

"We'll do that tomorrow," he said. "It's late now." He pulled the truck off the side of the road in a wide spot next to a field and turned off the headlights. He leaned over and undid their seatbelt, then looked at Riley. "Willow, can you just wait outside for a minute while I get your sister settled in?"

Suddenly, Riley knew they had to get away. It didn't matter that it was almost dark. Being in the dark was better than being in here.

Slowly, Riley opened the passenger door, then grabbed Mia, startling her awake. She lifted her sister over her lap and placed her down on the step. "Run, Mia, run!"

Mia jumped down from the truck and started to run, then turned and looked back at Riley, confused. Riley threw out her backpack and tried to follow Mia, but Todd had hold of her shirt.

"You brat!" he yelled, pulling her back into the cab.

Riley spun around and kicked as hard as she could. He shoved her feet aside. "Fine then, I'll teach you a lesson," he said, grabbing her legs so tight she thought her bones might snap.

"Stop! You're hurting me!" Riley yelled.

She needed to do something quick but what? Riley flung her arms back, trying to find something she could grab hold of. Suddenly, she felt something small and hard pressed into her hand. She forgot about everything else. Grandma's mace!

Riley shoved the tiny spray can in Todd's face, held her breath, and pushed the plunger. The can hissed and her eyes started burning. She squeezed her eyes shut tight.

"Ahhh!" Todd jerked away, releasing Riley's legs and digging at his eyes with his fists. "What did you do, you brat?"

"Take that, sucker!" Mia said somewhere behind Riley's back. Riley kicked away from Todd and scrambled out of the truck. She grabbed Mia's hand, snatched her backpack from the ground, and they ran. Riley's eyes burned so bad she could hardly see where they were going.

"Look," Mia said, pulling Riley to a stop. There was a fence with sharp pointy wire in front of them.

Riley wiped her eyes and glanced back over her shoulder at the truck. No sign of Todd, but they needed to get as far away as they could. Carefully, she grabbed the wire closest to the ground and pulled the wire high to make a space for Mia to crawl under then tossed the backpack after her. Riley slowly let the wire back down, then tried to squeeze through herself. The pointy wire ripped at her legs and grabbed hold of her shirt. Her heart stopped as she pictured Todd's hand grabbing her again, but he was still back in the truck yelling cuss words. Riley took a deep breath, reached back, and unhooked the wire from her shirt. Then she stood and grabbed Mia's hand.

"I know who you are," Todd yelled. Riley glanced back at the truck. He was standing in the light coming from the passenger side of the truck. There was something dark in his hand. Was it a gun? Was he going to shoot them? "If you don't come back now, I'll call the cops." He wiped his eyes with his sleeve, and Riley could see the gun clearly. "You little brat. You can't hide from me. I'll get you sooner or later."

"Run," Riley yelled and they took off through the field. They ran as long as they could, tripping over the field's uneven surface in the dark.

"I...can't..." Mia flopped to the ground and lay there panting. The air smelled of hay and plowed dirt. Riley stood beside her sister and tried to catch her breath. A large dark spot loomed in front of them—was it a building?

"Come on. Just a little further." Riley helped Mia up, then walked cautiously forward, keeping Mia behind her. As they got closer, she could see what she thought was a building was really a big stack of hay. Riley had seen small bales of hay before but this was like a rolled mountain of hay or a giant wheel of hay. The girls hid behind the stack and peeked out in the direction of the truck. Riley's heart pounded as Mia made little whimpering noises.

Was Todd out there looking for them? Would he shoot them both? Or worse, kill her and take Mia?

A truck engine rumbled from the direction of the road and lights flashed on. They were further away from the road than she'd thought. The truck pulled onto the highway and continued the direction they'd been going.

Riley let out a breath. Was he leaving for good or going to get the cops? And what were they going to do now?

CHAPTER ELEVEN

RILEY'S EYES had stopped watering though they still burned a little. Stars twinkled overhead. She glanced at the dark shapes scattered around the field, looking like monsters in the night. More wheels of hay? Riley shivered, but the monsters in the field weren't as frightening as the one in the truck. She took Mia's hand and they started walking, slower this time, feeling their way in the dark. Mia was still whimpering.

"Are you okay?" Riley asked, bending close to her sister.

"Is Todd going to hurt us?"

"I would never let anyone one hurt you, you know that. You were amazing back there, Mia. You saved us! What made you remember the mace?"

"He was trying to hurt you," Mia said in a small voice. Riley reached down and lifted her sister into her arms. Mia wrapped her legs tightly around Riley, burrowing her face in Riley's neck. "He was trying to hurt you," Mia said again.

Riley rocked back and forth, trying to comfort her sister. She wished River was with them.

"I've got to put you down. Mia. You're too heavy. Let's go just a little farther into the field, okay? Then we'll find somewhere to sleep."

Mia clung to Riley's hand as they walked quietly in the darkness, passing different-sized piles of hay. The ground changed under their feet, going from soft to hard. Riley squinted at the ground. It looked like they'd come to a dirt road. Another dark giant loomed ahead, looking slightly different than the mounds of hay. When they neared it, they realized it was a truck full of regular bales of hay. Riley walked around, peering at the empty cab and the bales of hay piled behind the cab.

"If we can crawl up on top of those bales, we'll be able to see the road," Riley whispered. "We can sleep up there and be safe." She lifted Mia up onto the hood of the truck. "Now climb onto the roof, then on top of the hay."

Mia scrambled up onto the hay and Riley followed her up. From this point she could see car lights on the highway in both direction for miles and miles.

Mia screamed.

"What?" Riley said, jumping to her feet.

"My backpack... Mr. Witherspoon! I left him in the truck," Mia wailed.

"Oh, Mia. I'm so sorry." Riley's heart raced as she pulled Mia close and held her tight. "I'll buy you another one, I promise."

"I—don't—want—another one!" Mia said between sobs. "I want my Mr. Witherspoon."

Riley held her crying sister until Mia was worn out. "I'll tell you a story," Riley said and then repeated the lines she had memorized from Mia's *Amelia Bedelia* book. The book was gone, but she knew the story by heart and Mia drifted off to the sound of the comforting words.

Sleep did not come quickly to Riley. She startled at every unfamiliar noise and kept an eye on the highway in case the trucker came back or the police came to take them away. The hay was fragrantly sweet but itchy on her skin, and the night air was getting colder. The bales weren't stacked tightly. She put her feet into the crack between bales and pushed over and over until she'd created a space large enough to fit the two of them. She woke Mia enough to get her down into the space, then pulled her sister close and covered them both with Riley's sweatshirt. Now that Mia's backpack was gone, she had no other clothes. At least it was warmer down between the bales.

Riley stared up at the stars, thinking about all the mistakes and wrong choices she'd made that day:

not turning themselves in when they had the chance, stealing the shampoo even though she hadn't meant to, and—worst of all—trusting that *man* even when she'd had an uh-oh feeling in her stomach. And now Mia's backpack was gone.

She was supposed to be taking care of Mia. Her grandma's voice had grown slowly silent while they were at Burning Man, but now it came rushing back. *Look what you've done now, you stupid, stupid kid.*

It seemed to take forever, but finally, Riley fell into a troubled sleep.

CHAPTER TWELVE

IN HER DREAMS, Riley heard the roar of the truck engine and felt the *uh-oh* in her stomach again. But then the scene changed. She was being held by her mother. She could smell her mother's sweet, fresh fragrance and feel her warm arms as they gently rocked together. She could hear her mother's soft voice singing her favorite lullaby...

Someone screamed and Riley jolted upright. Mia was standing with her arms out to her sides. "Riley, we're flying!"

Riley looked around and realized Mia was right. They were moving down the highway on the back of the hay truck with cow pastures flying by on either side.

How had she slept through the truck starting? Which direction were they going, back to Wells or further into Idaho?

She pulled Mia back down into their sleeping crevice. "We have to stay out of sight. What if someone sees us and calls the police?"

Mia frowned but stayed put. Riley smiled at her sister's funny braids all speckled with hay. She pulled a piece of hay out of Mia's hair and let it fly into the wind above them. Mia thought this was a great game. She pulled hay from the bales around her, then held the hay high and let it fly away.

What if we're going the wrong way? Riley wondered.

No use getting all pissy about it, as Grandma used to say. If they were going the wrong way, they would eventually hit the town called Jackpot. Instead of miles of sagebrush and cow pastures, Riley began to see small farms stretching out on either side of the road. She knew she had not seen this area before.

The air had a strong smell that made her nose hurt. Mia held her nose and grimaced. Riley pointed as they passed a place with hundreds of cows and Mia nodded.

Soon houses rose up on both sides along with stores and more people. Riley kept her head down and made sure Mia kept hers down, too.

Suddenly, the truck rumbled to a stop. Riley took a quick peek—they were in front of a feed store. She watched as the driver, a Mexican man with bent legs and a cowboy hat, walked inside the store. Then she put her finger to her lips and signaled for Mia to follow her. They climbed down onto the roof and over the opposite side of the truck. Once down on the asphalt parking lot, Riley took Mia's hand and moved rapidly away from the truck before stopping to look around.

They were in a much bigger town than Wells, but not as big as Reno. The buildings were small and looked really old. Across the street was some kind of store. Riley headed that way, hoping for a bathroom with a sink to fill their water bottles. Her water bottle, she corrected herself. Mia's was lost with her backpack.

The morning sun beat down on them as they waited to cross the street. She started to sweat and her skin itched from sleeping in the hay. The shower in Wells felt like it had happened a week ago, not a day ago.

This town smelled different than Reno. Reno smelled like sage. This town smelled like those cows they'd seen earlier. There were lots of cars and pickups with drivers wearing cowboy hats. Riley had seen a few cowboys before in Reno but never so many.

A bell jingled as they entered the store with a sign that said "Goodwill" over the door. Cold air hit them and Riley began to shiver. From the look and smell, they were in a thrift store. Mama used to buy all their clothes from thrift stores when they were little. "It's a small planet," Mama used to say. "If we all shared our stuff, everyone would have enough."

The cash register was to their right and Riley dragged Mia over to it. The woman behind the counter was as old as Grandma, but skinnier and had her hair piled up on her head like a fancy cake. Riley was staring at the woman's impossibly unmoving hair when the woman said, "Can I help you?"

"Uh...do you have a bathroom we can use?" Riley stammered.

The woman gave her a hard look. With their dusty clothes and messy hair they must look like runaways. What if this woman had seen their faces on TV? Riley's stomach knotted.

"Are you planning to buy anything today?" The woman's voice was sweet but her manner was all business.

"Of course," Riley said quickly. "Do you have food here?"

"No, dear. This is a *thrift* store, but there's a Tasty Freeze down the street."

"Well, we're here to buy..." Riley glanced around, eyes landing on racks of clothes, "a shirt."

"Then go ahead and use the bathroom, dear. It's back in the corner by the toys." The woman pointed a bony finger at the back right section of the store.

"Thank you," Riley said and turned Mia in that direction. Then Riley stopped. She didn't want to act like a runaway, but they had to know where they were. She turned back and asked, "Um, could you remind me what the name of this city is?"

"The name of this city?" The woman repeated, looking as if she'd heard wrong.

"Yes," Riley said, thinking hard. Maybe if she sounded like a cowgirl, she'd be less suspicious. "We're here visitin' our cousin and I up and forgot the name of this here city."

Mia frowned and looked confused.

The woman's eyes widened, then her eyebrows bunched together. "Well now, it's Twin Falls, of course."

"Oh, that's right," Riley said, smacking her forehead with the heel of her hand. "And," she continued, "how far would you say we are from..." She pulled the sealed envelope from her back pocket and read the address. "Wen-dell, Idaho?"

The woman tilted her head and narrowed her eyes. "Wendell's about thirty miles up the road. Why do you ask?"

"Well...Ma'am, I have a..." She tried to think of something to say. Then she remembered a story her grandma had told her about a friend she used to exchange letters with. "I have a pen pal that lives in Wendell and was just wonderin' where that is."

The woman nodded. "I'm glad to hear that. Very few people write letters these days. I had a pen pal when I was your age. I hope you get a chance to visit her while you're here. Where are you girls from?"

Mia piped up. "I'm from San Francisco!" she said with a flourish, her arms stretched out from her sides, her knee bent.

Riley looked at her sister with surprise. Mia had introduced herself that way to grownups when she was little and had always gotten a laugh, but Riley thought she'd forgotten all about it.

The woman didn't laugh, but nodded as if that explained everything.

The bell jangled, announcing new customers. Riley took hold of Mia's hand and headed through the toy section to the bathroom. Once inside, she realized the room must double as a dressing room. It had a full-length mirror. They stood in front of the mirror inspecting their reflections.

Mia mimicked Grandma's raspy voice. "Well, look what the cat dragged in. You two look like sh—" Riley clamped her hand over Mia's mouth before she could finish one of Grandma's colorful sayings. Mia's eyes sparkled over the almost-said bad word and Riley couldn't help but smile back.

Riley lowered her hand from Mia's mouth and placed a quick kiss on her forehead. "Let's see what we can do to clean up. We just might meet my dad today and we can't meet him looking like this."

She dampened a paper towel with water and tried to clean Mia's face, then decided they both needed to get rid of their braids — the night in the hay had left them frazzled. She undid her own braids first, leaving her hair kinked all the way down, then untied Mia's braids. Mia's hair fell about her shoulders in silky waves. She and Mia stared at her reflection, their mouths open in wonder.

"Mia! I think we've found a way to tame your hair. It looks...fantastic."

Mia glowed, turning around and around to get a better view in the mirror. Riley counted their bag of change—seven dollars. She didn't think they could afford both clothes and lunch. They would have to sneak out without buying a shirt. She felt bad for having lied to the woman, but there wasn't anything she could do about it now.

When Riley opened the bathroom door, Mia shrieked and Riley's heart jumped into her throat. She glanced around, looking to see what had scared her sister. Had the trucker come back for them like he promised? Or had the woman called the police? She tried to pull the door closed, but Mia pushed past her and rushed over to the shelves of stuffed animals.

"It's Mr. Witherspoon!" Mia said, clutching a teddy bear to her chest.

CHAPTER THIRTEEN

THE TEDDY BEAR turned out to be Mr. Witherspoon—or close enough to be his twin. Mia wouldn't leave the store without him so Riley had to part with a precious dollar. Then they walked to the Tasty Freeze and waited for it to open.

Mia spun a complicated tale about how Mr. Witherspoon had escaped from the evil truck driver and traveled across country in cars of helpful boys and girls to find Mia again. Riley stared at the menu hanging in the window, trying to decide how best to spend their limited cash. She had to buy food for Mia. She didn't need any for herself but Mia had to eat. The last real meal they'd eaten had been the pizza in Wells. And Todd had shared some potato chips with them in the truck. Riley shivered, glancing around quickly to make sure he was nowhere around.

She decided the best deal was a six-dollar value meal that came with a hamburger, fries, and a coke.

Her stomach growled. Maybe I'll just have a couple bites, she decided.

Riley stacked the change from her plastic bag in small piles to make sure they had enough. With a sigh of relief she realized they would have almost a dollar left over. A dollar was not much when you still had thirty miles to go.

How would they get to Wendell? Would there be another bus they could hide in? Maybe she could find someone nice like Hubcap to give them a ride. But what if it turned out to be someone mean like Todd? Could she find another hay truck?

Riley's thoughts went round and round without really getting anywhere. It was a relief when the Tasty Freeze finally opened and they could place their order.

All ideas of taking only a few bites went out the window when Riley smelled the hamburger cooking on the grill. Her mouth watered and her stomach growled even louder. When the order came she cut the hamburger down the middle and counted out the fries, giving Mia an extra fry so Riley didn't feel quite so guilty about eating half. The pizza in Wells had been wonderful, but this hamburger was delicious!

TWO HOURS LATER Riley still hadn't figured out how they were going to get to Wendell. It was so hot even the shade of the Tasty Freeze awning wasn't enough.

Mia was getting tired and cranky and complaining again about needing to go to the bathroom. The man at behind the Tasty Freeze counter said their bathroom was only for employees, so Riley led her sister back towards the thrift store. The best luck she'd had on this trip had come when she asked River for help. They needed help again and the only person she knew to ask was the cashier.

Riley even had a plan. A plan that might work, or might land them right in the place they'd been trying to avoid — the shelter. It might be a good time to pray, but Riley didn't know much about prayer. Her mom had said it was easiest to hear God in the forest or at the ocean, but Riley couldn't see either one from where she was. She tried to picture what the forest or ocean looked like, but her memories of both were fuzzy. The oppressive heat burned her head and radiated up from the sidewalk.

"God," she whispered under her breath, desperate as she pulled Mia into the thrift store. "We need a ride to my dad's house. And, please...make it a safe one."

Once inside the store they both groaned in relief as cool air washed over them. The store was full of customers. Riley wondered how many were there to shop and how many were there to cool off. She took Mia to the bathroom first, then approached the woman at the cash register with the cake-like hairdo. They had to wait their turn in line behind a woman so wide Riley and Mia could stand side by side behind her and no one would see them. Riley hoped Mia didn't get any bright ideas about hugging this woman like she had hugged the large woman who'd made them breakfast at Burning Man.

When the large woman's bulging bags were handed to her, Riley stepped up and gave the cashier her most pleasant smile.

The bone-thin woman smiled down at them. "Well, if it isn't stuff and nonsense! You coming to return the bear?"

Mia clutched Mr. Witherspoon tightly to her chest.

"No," Riley said quickly. "We were wondering if you knew any safe people in your store who might be going to Wendell."

The woman stared at her as if her words made no sense. She repeated slowly, "You want to know if I know any safe people to give you a ride to Wendell?"

"Yes," Riley said and grinned again. How does Mia pull off charming so easily? Riley wondered as her cheeks began to ache from smiling.

The cashier glanced down the growing line of people. "You want to go see your pen pal?" she asked.

"Well, maybe," Riley said, repeating the line she'd practiced at the Tasty Freeze. "Actually, my

Grandma also lives over there and my aunt was going to take us today, but her car broke and she said if we could get a ride, she'd come get us tomorrow."

Riley held her breath, hoping this was a good enough story, while the cashier took a pencil from behind her ear and used it to scratch her head up inside the cake hairdo. The cashier glanced at the line again and Riley looked back. Five people. An old lady caught Riley's eye and frowned.

"Hey, Betty May," the clerk said. "How you doing today?"

"My ankles are starting to swell from the heat and standing here's not helping," the old lady said. The cashier frowned as another person joined the line. She turned back to Riley. "I don't have time to help you figure this out, girls. My line's backing up. Jack..." she said loudly to the second man in line. His head jerked up.

This man had to be the oldest person Riley had ever seen. The cashier spoke loudly and slowly while Riley stared. He reminded her of a turtle she had once seen at a zoo on a field trip. Her teacher read the plaque out loud to the class—the turtle was over a hundred years old. It had a long wrinkly neck and a bald head, just like this man Jack.

"Jack! These girls need a ride to Wendell. Can you help them figure it out? Call their aunt."

Jack looked down at the girls and up at the cashier. Without a word he shuffled out of the line and headed toward the door, carrying a shirt he had not yet purchased.

"The shirt, Jack!" yelled the cashier.

Jack shuffled back to the counter and handed the shirt to the cashier, then shambled away again.

The cashier shook her head and turned to the next customer. Jack kept walking right toward the front door, so Riley grabbed Mia's hand and followed. He kept going out into the parking lot and stopped at a green car that looked even older than the one Hubcap drove. He didn't turn around or say a word. Did he even know she and Mia were following him?

Finally, he opened the passenger door. "Sorry, we have no air conditioning." He spoke in a loud voice, but not slow like the clerk had.

Riley stopped. She didn't have any *uh-oh* feelings about Jack. Besides, he was so old and frail she and Mia could get away from him in a heartbeat. But his driving ability was another matter. He looked like he should be sitting in a rocker, not driving a car. Mia looked up at her, a worried expression on her face.

Jack held the door open while the girls slid in. Riley sat in the middle between Jack and Mia, just in case she was wrong about him. Jack closed the passenger door, then took forever getting over to his side of the car. They might just be dead from the heat by the time he got in the car.

He finally shut the driver's door. "Roll down your winda. Let's get some air flowing here."

Riley looked for a button to push and could find none. She watched the old man crank the window down with a hand crank attached to the door. She leaned across Mia and cranked down their window as far as it would go. It seemed like it took forever for Jack to get his seatbelt fastened. It took all the patience Riley had left not to rip that seatbelt from his hands and do it herself.

"We're going to Wendell, right?" Riley shouted.

"What?" asked Jack. "I'm a little deaf; you'll have to speak up."

"We're going to Wendell, right?" Riley yelled as loud as she could.

"Wendell? I'm from Wendell. No problem at all. I'll have you there lickety split."

Riley sat back against the seat, relieved. At least they were going the right direction. But as Jack backed the car out of the parking space Riley started to have second thoughts. Jack looked and walked like a turtle, but drove like a maniac. Gravel sprayed as he peeled out onto the road, nearly missing an oncoming car that had to swerve quickly to avoid hitting them. Jack smiled. He seemed happily unaware that his action had cut off another driver. Mia grabbed

Riley's hand and they clutched each other tightly. The big car swerved down the road at an alarming rate. Once again, Riley could hear Grandma's raspy voice in her head, *You've done it this time, you good-for-nothing girl.*

Chapter Fourteen

I T WAS NO USE trying to talk to Jack. Riley gave it one more try after he turned onto the highway and left his blinker on. She shouted and pointed at the blinker, but between the wind howling through the windows and his deafness, she couldn't make herself heard, so she finally stopped trying. Jack seemed content with the silence. He was probably used to it.

After a time Mia's grip loosened on Riley's hand and Riley realized her sister was asleep. How anyone could sleep when they might die in a fiery crash was beyond her.

What if a cow wandered onto the road? What if a tractor pulled out or they hit a pothole? Any one of these things could kill them. She hardly breathed during the thirty long miles to Wendell.

When Jack screeched into the parking lot of an old store in a tiny town, Riley breathed a huge sigh of relief. Was this Wendell? Mia jolted awake as dust boiled up around them.

"Let me buy you a coke. It's a real blazer out there," Jack said.

Maybe this wasn't Wendell, after all. They slowly followed Jack into the tiny store. Riley stared at the fans blowing all the hot air around.

"Why don't they have air conditioning?" Mia asked. Riley shook her head and put a finger to her lips. She brushed a fly off her arm, then another one off her face.

"Hey, Jack. Who you got there?" yelled a friendly-looking man behind the counter.

"I got me a couple strays," Jack said with a grin. "Thought they might need a coke after that dusty ride in from town."

The man took two cokes from a refrigerator and placed them on the counter. "They probably need more than a coke after riding with you, Jack!" Both men laughed. Riley noticed that Jack kept his eyes on the man's face when he talked and seemed to be able to hear better that way. Maybe that's why he couldn't hear me in the car, Riley thought. He couldn't read my lips.

Jack turned to Riley. "What's the address yer lookin' for?" he asked.

Riley pulled the worn envelope out of her back pocket and handed it to Jack. Her nose tickled from drinking the soda so fast.

Mia began to wander around the small store as Jack studied the address, then leaned over the counter and showed it to the friendly man. The store clerk's eyebrows rose up causing deep lines, like spines of stacked books, to form across his forehead. Then he and Jack exchanged a look. Riley's heart sank. Was this the end of the road? Did the whole town know her father didn't want her? Had they been warned to send her away if she came looking for him?

Jack asked, "So you're going to see your Grandma, eh?"

Riley glanced at him, confused for a moment. She'd been so worried about what was going to happen, she'd forgotten the lie she'd told in the thrift store. Jack had to have heard her talking to the clerk—she hadn't mentioned visiting her grandma during the ride here. Had she?

"Yes," Riley answered, her head down. Then she remembered he couldn't hear her that way and looked into his eyes. "Yes."

"Well, this here envelope is addressed to Blaine Baker," he said, a question in his voice. He waited.

Riley didn't know how much to tell Jack so she just nodded.

"Blaine doesn't live here anymore." Jack stated matter-of-factly. His words sent an avalanche of pain and dread tumbling down to crush Riley's soul. She suddenly felt exhausted, as if all the energy she had expended to get them here had left her body all at once. She felt Mia slip up beside her, taking her hand. Of all the things she had imagined—her father not wanting her, her father telling her to go back home, her father not believing she was even his daughter—she'd never thought they had come all this way only to find he wasn't here. Her eyes filled with tears and her throat closed up. She blinked rapidly, not wanting Mia to see her pain.

Jack continued, "He moved up north in the Sawtooth about ten years back, married a cute little gal up there."

The Sawtooth? Suddenly, Riley felt like she'd been pushed as high as she could go on a swing, and if she just let go at the right time, she would actually fly. If she gotten them this far, maybe she could get them to the Sawtooth—even though she had no idea where or what that was. All she had to do was hang on a little longer, though her whole body trembled at the thought.

"Your grandma's here, though. The reason this letter didn't get to her is 'cause this address is off a bit. She has a farm down the road. She know you're coming?"

The question took a minute to sink in. Her grandma? She really had another grandma? Maybe they wouldn't have to walk to the Sawtooth, after all.

Riley was so relieved she almost forgot she'd lied to Jack in the first place. "Sure," she said. "She's expecting us."

Jack and the man behind the counter exchanged another look. Riley squeezed Mia's hand, took an oversized cowboy hat off her sister's head, and handed the hat to the man behind the counter.

"Well, pile into the old rocket, then," Jack said. "We'll be there in a flash. See ya later, Toby." Jack nodded at the other man, opened the door, and headed back into the blasting heat.

Toby called a hearty goodbye, but Riley's mind was still reeling. They were going to meet her Grandma! Her heart skipped a beat as she and Mia shared a grin as they skipped out the door.

Chapter Fifteen

J ACK SLOWED THE CAR as they approached a gravel driveway that looked like every other gravel driveway they'd passed. Riley touched his arm and he brought the car to sudden stop, throwing the girls forward. He turned toward Riley, raising an eyebrow in question.

"Is that my Grandma's house?" she shouted, pointing across a hay field to a small white house in the distance.

"That's it."

Riley looked at the house and her stomach tied itself into little knots. She wanted to tell Jack she'd changed her mind. What if this grandma didn't want them? What if this grandma was just like the grandma they'd left dead in bed?

She looked down at Mia. Her sister's face had lost the sparkle it usually had. Little Mia, once full of life and joy, now looked small and scared. Her eyes had dark circles under them. They'd been through a lot in the last twenty-four hours. She couldn't drag Mia through more uncertainty with the possibility of a bed and food and a family so close. "Jack, do you mind if we walk in from here?"

"Are you sure, sweetie?"

"Yes."

Jack sat, looking at Riley as if trying to decide what was best. Finally, he ruffled her hair with a hand as light as a bird's wing.

"If that's the way you want it." He slowly opened the door and shuffled around to the girls' side of the car. Riley waited patiently, wondering if maybe she should have him drive them to the house after all. That way, if this grandma started yelling...

Jack opened the door, cupped each girl's chin in his feather-light hands, and looked at their faces.

"You'll be fine," he assured them. "LaRue's not the softest gal in town, but she'd never turn away kin."

Both girls flew into his arms, almost knocking him down. Riley felt such relief from his words she didn't want to let go. He was sturdier than he looked and smelled of peppermint and something sweet like oranges.

"Now, now," he said. "I'll check on you in a day or two." He bent down, placing a light kiss on the top of each girl's head and turned to go. He shambled to the other side of the car and then stopped.

"Watch out for Old Blue. He's an ornery cuss, but it's mostly show." Jack climbed into the driver's seat and turned the car around.

They waved as the old man hit the gas and quickly became a speck on the horizon. Riley turned to Mia. "Ready?"

Mia nodded, her face set in that stubborn look that usually made Riley cringe. Riley stuck out her hand and Mia took it, both girls resolutely turning down the lane to face their destiny.

Chapter Sixteen

T HE GRAVEL DRIVEWAY was long and lined with tall trees on the left side. To their right was a fence surrounding a field with baled hay. It was not a big pasture like they had walked through the night before, and the hay bales were not in big stacks but lay scattered around the field.

"I'm scared," Mia said.

"Of meeting Grandma?"

"No, of the dog."

They hadn't seen or heard Old Blue yet, but they both kept looking around. Mia's grip tightened on Riley's hand. The long driveway curved to the right when it reached another field. Riley counted five cows and three calves in the field in front of them. They walked along under the shady trees and Riley breathed a sigh of relief. It was so much easier to watch for the dog without the sun beating on her.

She relaxed. They could see the little white house clearly: a tall white fence framed the grassy yard around it and flowers lined the side of the fence. A breeze brought a mixture of smells toward them: sweet flowers, musty cows, and damp earth from the water she could hear running nearby. The fence ended in a closed gate that hung at a crooked angle.

A horrible screech split the air. It almost sounded like a baby screaming. Mia jumped and grabbed Riley's legs. Riley wrapped her arms protectively around her sister and looked frantically around. From somewhere behind them came a great whooshing sound and suddenly they were staring eye to eye with the biggest bird Riley had ever seen. The bird was dark blue and spread out the most amazing fan of tail feathers as it strutted back and forth in front of them, blocking their path to the house.

"What is it?" cried Mia.

"I'm not sure, but I think it might be Old Blue."

The bird kept screeching and pacing, coming closer and closer with each pass. Riley kept backing up with Mia behind her until they were pressed up against a tree in front of the cow pasture. There was no way to get around the huge bird. Had they come all this way only to be killed by a crazy bird?

"Blue!" someone yelled. Riley turned to see a woman striding toward them. Hair stood out around her head in a white halo. She was wearing blue coveralls and rubber waders that came up to her waist. Her voice was firm but not sharp.

"Down, boy. Go on now. Shoo, shoo." The woman walked right up to the squawking bird. It skittered away, flying to the top of the fence as if to keep an eye on them. The woman turned and looked both Riley and Mia up and down. Then she started to chuckle. The sound started as a small burble and grew louder and louder, until she was slapping her knees and wiping at tears.

Riley didn't know what to think. Was this her grandma or a crazed farm worker? Maybe she should drag Mia back up the lane as fast as they could run.

When the woman stopped laughing, she held up a hand. "I'm sorry. It's just that my attack peacock has treed a lot of things in his time, but nothing quite as pitiful looking as you two."

She chuckled some more and Riley wondered if she was about to start up again. Instead she asked, "You two lost? You visitin' over at Zeek and Zelda's place?"

This was the moment Riley had been waiting for, hoping for, working for, and suddenly she had no words. The woman stared at her, waiting for an answer. Finally, Mia elbowed her in the leg.

"Ow!" Riley took a breath and reached into her back pocket. She held the envelope toward the woman who reached out and took it gingerly.

The woman pulled a small pair of reading glasses from the bib pocket of her coveralls and looked at the envelope.

"Well, this is addressed to my son Blaine," she said as if Riley didn't know. "This was sent eleven years ago and to the wrong address. Who's it from?"

"My mom," Riley said, suddenly feeling shy.

Her grandmother looked at her for a long time. Then she ripped open the letter, pulled a single pink sheet of stationery out, and held it up to the fading light. Her head tilted to one side as she read.

Riley had always wondered what the letter said, but never felt like she should open it. What had her mother said? Her stomach twisted. What would her Grandma do after she finished reading the letter? Would she send them away?

Grandma looked at Riley, then at Mia, then back at Riley. "You must be Riley."

Tears sprang to Riley's eyes. She blinked hard to keep them back. She swallowed a lump in her throat and nodded, but it seemed her grandmother wanted something more.

"This is my sister, Mia."

"You can call me Nana," the woman said. "The rest all do." She nodded and swept her hand toward the house. "I imagine you two are hungry. Little ones always are, and from the looks of things, you have a story to tell." She walked to the old gate, unlatching it and letting it swing open, uneven on its hinges.

Riley and Mia looked at each other. Mia's eyes sparkled as she hopped the first hop Riley had seen in what felt like forever. Mia skipped happily toward the house and Riley rushed to follow, keeping an eye on the mean bird. They walked on stepping stones almost buried by the surrounding grass. Suddenly, Mia darted to the right and stopped at the edge of the grass where the flowers began. She was standing by a huge silver bell, half her own height.

"It's okay," Nana said. "Give it a push. You have to pull hard to get it to work."

Mia pushed the silver lever back and forth until the bell gave a reluctant ring and then clanged over and over. Mia laughed, delighted. Riley breathed a sigh of relief. It was good to see Mia's playfulness return.

Riley watched as Grandma, no...Nana climbed up several steps to the porch which was just long enough to hold two rocking chairs. She pulled off the rubber waders. "You two caught me cleaning out the irrigation ditch—a chore I certainly don't mind being interrupted from." Her voice was stern, but had the feeling of a smile behind it, like a teacher who tries to appear strict to her students but you can tell she really likes them. Mrs. Taylor was like that, and she was Riley's favorite.

Nana opened the screen door and waved the girls inside. Riley still couldn't believe this was happening.

Her heart pounded so hard she was sure Nana could hear it. They were in what looked like a dining area. A small table sat off to their left, covered in a white plastic tablecloth with little blue flowers all over it. A counter separated the dining area from the kitchen.

"I like your house," Mia said.

"Oh, this old place? Why, it ain't nothing but a shanty on a sand hill. But I guess I like it all right. Now, when was the last time you two ate something?"

Riley thought for a moment. "We split a hamburger and fries this morning."

"At the Tasty Freeze!" Mia clapped her hands and grinned.

"Well, that was two years ago in child time," Nana said. "I'd better see what we have to feed you." She went into the kitchen and soon had white plates with blue flowers on the table and platters of sliced roast beef, chicken, cheese, and cookies filling up the center. She poured large glasses of milk. Riley hadn't realized how much she missed drinking milk until she took the first swallow and didn't stop until the glass was empty. Nana kept bringing out more food—cantaloupe, sliced tomatoes and peas fresh from the garden—and they kept eating. When Riley thought she was going to pop, Nana brought out thick slices of chocolate cake.

Riley sat back in her chair, stomach bulging. The sun had set and crickets and frogs began to croak and chirp. She loved the unfamiliar sound—it was so peaceful. Mia's eyes started to droop.

"I'm only going to ask you one question tonight," Nana said. "Then, it's off to the bath while I try to find some pajamas you might fit in. We'll talk about the rest tomorrow. For right now, I just need to know one thing: Is there anyone I need to call and let know you're here?" She gave Riley a serious look.

"No one," Riley said, equally serious.

"All right then, let's get you scrubbed up and off to bed." Nana led them through the kitchen to a small room that contained two of the biggest sinks Riley had ever seen. To their right was a small bathroom with a tub and a shower.

"You girls want a bath or shower?"

"Bath," they replied at once. Riley couldn't remember the last time they'd had a nice hot bath. Their other grandma had never let them use her bath, saying it took too much water, and the shelter didn't have a bathtub. Had their old house had one? She couldn't even remember now. She was so tired and it seemed a long time ago.

Nana surprised them by pouring a bunch of bubble bath into the tub. "Looks like you two could use some extra soap and you might as well enjoy it."

She laid out towels and showed Riley where the shampoo and conditioner was, handing them soft wash clothes and then closing the door.

The girls wasted no time stripping out of their dusty clothes and slipping into the warm bubbles. Riley giggled and splashed, feeling as young as Mia as they laughed and played and scrubbed away their dirt. Nana tapped on the door, then pushed it open a crack.

"I found some pajamas that I think will work," she said, entering the bathroom with her back to them and placing a small stack of clothes on the toilet seat before slipping back out the door. Riley washed Mia's hair and Mia washed Riley's. When they got out, Riley braided Mia's hair so it would look pretty in the morning. Riley pulled on t-shirts and shorts that seemed to belong to a boy and Mia pulled a flannel nightgown over her head.

Nana tucked them into twin beds in what she called the guest room. "All right, you two wild things," she said, still standing at the door. "I'll see you in the morning." She flipped off the light and pulled the door almost closed.

As soon as her footsteps moved away, Mia got out of her bed and crawled in with Riley. They'd been sleeping together too long to change tonight. Mia was asleep before her head hit the pillow. Riley didn't know what would happen tomorrow, but tonight they'd eaten and were clean and safe.

CHAPTER SEVENTEEN

RILEY WOKE UP to the smell of bacon and the sound of someone talking on the phone. It took her awhile to remember where she was. Mia was asleep beside her so she held still, listening.

"Well, I don't think it's a good idea for everyone to rush over here. These little ones look like kittens in a rain gutter. Blaine an' Delly will be here as soon as they can, once they get done moving cows up to the high pasture."

Riley sat up—Blaine was coming. Her dad was coming! She placed her hand over her chest to try and quiet her pounding heart. What would he be like? Would he like her? Would he want to keep her? What would they do if he didn't let them stay?

Riley squeezed her eyes shut tight, then opened them. Maybe Nana would let them stay here if her dad didn't want them. It seemed like a nice place, except for that devil bird.

Nana peeked around the door. "I gotta go," she said into the phone. "One of the kittens is awake and hungry, no doubt." She clicked off the cell phone, stepped into the room, and shoved the phone in the back pocket of her jeans.

"Good morning, Miss Riley. Did you sleep well?"

Riley nodded, unsure of what to say.

"I see you have company."

"We're used to sleeping together."

Nana stood as if waiting for more but Riley said nothing.

"Well, see if you can't wake Sleeping Beauty there, and I'll finish up making breakfast." Nana headed out of the room without another word.

Mia was sleeping so peacefully Riley hated to wake her. This bed was the softest she could remember and smelled fresh. It was much better than hay stacks, Burner couches, and the thin, lumpy mattress of their old foldout bed. Too bad they couldn't just lay here forever. But she could hear Nana clanging around in the kitchen so Riley began her wake-up song.

BREAKFAST WAS AMAZING: fried steak, fried potatoes, fried eggs, cinnamon rolls, and orange juice. Maybe Nana was used to cooking for a lot of people. She sure had a ton of food around. The girls ate as much as they could, but couldn't finish it all.

"After I wash up these dishes, I'll show you around the farm," Nana said. "Not much of a farm anymore really. I've sold off most of it. Just ten acres left but I always like to walk it in the morning and check on everything. Then we'll come in for coffee and cookies and you can tell me your story. You girls like coffee?"

Riley and Mia looked at each other and grinned. Mia giggled. "We've never had coffee. We're kids!"

Nana chuckled. "Well, who's to say a kid can't have a little coffee? It's good for ya. Puts hair on your chest."

Mia's eyes grew wide and she pulled the top of her shirt out to look down.

Nana started laughing again—a loud, long laugh that made Mia and Riley laugh too. "I'll load up these dishes and you two go get dressed. I washed your things last night but looks like you two might need some new clothes. Maybe we'll take a drive into Twin tomorrow." She rose, gathering plates to carry into the kitchen.

Riley turned to Mia and wondered if her eyes were as wide and full of hope as her sister's. If Nana wanted to buy them clothes, maybe she wouldn't send them away to the shelter if her dad didn't want them. Maybe she'd keep them instead.

"Go get dressed now," Nana said, coming back for more dishes. "Your clothes are in the bathroom and I set out some toothbrushes and a hairbrush for you. I threw your old brush away. I don't know where you were to get everything that dirty. Now, let's skedaddle! Morning's a wastin'."

The girls jumped up, raced to the bathroom, and pulled on their clothes as fast as they could. They brushed their teeth—which was hard to do because they couldn't stop smiling. Riley unbraided Mia's hair and it fell in lovely waves. Riley's hair stuck up funny from going to bed with it wet. She put a little water on her hair and brushed it down as best she could.

"Let's go, you two," Nana said as she passed the bathroom and headed out the back of the house. They walked through a room that Riley thought must be the laundry room. Off to the left were stairs going down into the dark.

"What's down there?" asked Mia

"Oh, that's where I keep my canning and extra food."

Now I know where all the food keeps coming from, Riley thought.

They went out a back door. When they got outside Mia ran up and grabbed Nana's hand. Nana stopped and held out her other hand. Riley hesitated, then reached out and slipped her hand into Nana's.

The lawn wrapped around the back of the house, and beyond the lawn was the field they'd passed on the way in. Their feet sank into the wet grass as they passed a large chicken coop with hens pecking around the grass beside it. The sharp smell of chickens stung Riley's nose.

Nana nodded at the coop. "I already pulled the eggs this morning but maybe you can help me tomorrow." Riley didn't think she'd like getting closer to that smell.

Behind the house was the biggest garden Riley had ever seen. Nana showed them huge tomatoes, corn, lettuce, beans, and other plants. She seemed to be especially proud of her garden, pulling ripe vegetables from the vines and handing them to the girls. Once they were through in the garden, Nana led them back across the lawn to some small buildings.

"Here's my workshop," Nana said, pointing at a small white building the size of a large playhouse. "I like to work with wood."

They passed a large barn with cars in it—a jeep and a pickup truck.

"What's that?" asked Mia for the millionth time, pointing at a small fenced area.

"That's a pen for the bull when he comes to visit."

Why would a bull want to visit a farm?

"What's that?" Mia asked, pointing to another barn on their left.

"That's the milking barn. Come on, I'll show you." Nana took them into a small building with four odd-looking machines standing in a row.

"What are those?" asked Mia

"Those are the machines I hook up to the cows to get the milk. I milked the girls this morning. Only two need milking right now as three have calves."

Then there was an irrigation ditch that ran through the property and lots of old farm equipment that Riley and Mia were allowed to climb up on. Nana seemed to think the farm wasn't much, with having sold most of it off to other people, but Riley thought it was about the most perfect place she'd ever seen. She dreamed of sitting in the sun, reading a book near the barn, while Mia played happily nearby.

It took about an hour to check on everything. Riley hadn't seen Old Blue and was glad for that. Nana pulled a weed, picked a wild berry, or cut off stalks of the wild asparagus growing along the fence as they walked along the lane. The girls had their arms full by the time they came back in the house. Riley thought there was no way she could be hungry again after such a big breakfast but when Nana filled their cups with warm milk, sugar, and a small drop of coffee, then set out cookies for dipping, Riley dug right in.

"Now," Nana said, settling in across from the girls with a full cup of black coffee in her hands. "Let's hear your story."

Nana didn't say much as Riley told their story with Mia helping out with the details. Nana frowned, shaking her head when Riley described finding Grandma dead and Riley's fear about the shelter. Her forehead wrinkled and she said "tisk tisk" when Mia described sneaking onto the bus. Her eyes widened as they told of their adventures at Burning Man, and her eyes flashed when they described their scary encounter with the truck driver. As they told of their escape from Todd she got up from her chair as if the story got too scary, even for her. She paced back and forth before pouring more coffee and then sitting back down. When they got to the part about Jack and his deafness and wild driving, she laughed so hard tears streamed down her cheeks.

When they were finished Nana sat staring off into space. Riley wasn't sure what to do next. Should she say something?

Nana shook her head as if to clear it. She looked at them. Riley held her breath—was Nana mad?

"Well, I need to do me some thinkin'," Nana finally said. "But I'll say one thing for sure. You are two of the bravest kittens I've ever met! I gotta hand that to you, I do."

Brave. Nana thought they were brave! The praise washed over Riley, feeling as good as when River gave her the name Willow.

Nana stood up. "Okay, you two go explore the farm while I think. Stay out of the ditch now; it can be dangerous. I think if you enter the barn quietly, you'll hear some little mews to the left. Ol' Harry surprised me by laying five kittens a few weeks ago. Guess I'll have to call her Harriet now." She laughed at her own joke. "If you approach her real slow and let her smell your hands, she'll let you hold the babies. Either that or scratch your eyes out." She laughed again. "Now go!" Nana swept her hands at them and the girls scampered for the front door.

CHAPTER EIGHTEEN

RILEY AND MIA shared a chair in the small living room that evening after dinner. Two people Nana had introduced as the sheriff and a social worker sat across from them on the couch. Nana sat in a rocking chair to their right. Nana had asked Riley to repeat their story and she did so in a voice so soft the sheriff asked her to speak up twice. Then she and Mia answered a seemingly endless amount of questions.

Now the sheriff, a man with red hair and a big forehead, held his hat in his hand, looking nervous. "Well, LaRue. I did some checking after you called and...you're right about the girls. All of Nevada is looking for 'em."

Riley grabbed Mia's hand and squeezed. What would happen now? Would they be arrested and put in jail for running away? Would Nana let the social worker take them to a shelter?

The social worker, a woman with graying hair wearing a brown pant suit, finally spoke up. "I've called Washoe County Social Services to assure them the girls are safe and well cared for, LaRue, but they might have to go back there until this all gets straightened out."

Riley's throat tightened. She wanted to speak out, to tell them they would not go back, but her grandmother beat her to it. Nana stood up and began pacing, "That's not going to happen, Judy. We're the only family these two have and I'll fight for 'em if I have to. They'll be just fine here while the whozits in Nevada figure things out."

"But, LaRue," the sheriff said. "We can't even be sure she's Blaine's daughter."

Nana turned and pointed her finger at his face. "Kenny Junior, you look at that child and tell me she's not Blaine's. You've known him since kindergarten. She's the spittin' image of my son and you know it."

The sheriff looked at Riley and nodded. Warmth flooded through Riley. She was scared, about as scared as she'd ever been, but now she knew something that made her spirits soar—she looked like her father. All her life Riley had felt out of place. Mia looked so much like their mother and was so much like her in personality while Riley was nothing like their mother. Now Riley knew where her looks came from. Was she like her father in other ways?

The social worker gestured at Mia. "But what about this one?"

Riley put her arm around Mia's shoulders. She would not let Mia be taken from her. Not even if she had to give up this farm and Nana and a father she'd never met but looked like.

"Look, Judy. If Mia had any other family, they would've been found when her parents died. She's staying here too."

The social worker nodded. "You're probably right about that." She stood and the sheriff stood, too. "You can keep them tonight 'cause I can vouch for you, but LaRue, there are rules and regulations in place for a reason. They're there to protect children and we have to follow them."

"I know that, Judy," Nana said. She didn't sound angry anymore. "I know you'll do your best to help us through this mess." She led the two through the kitchen and dining room to the front door. "You keep me posted now."

Nana came back in and sat in the middle of the small couch. She patted the cushions beside her. Riley and Mia ran to her side and she put her arms around them protectively. Riley snuggled up against Nana's strong body while Mia did the same on the other side.

"Don't worry, girls," she said, kissing each one on the top of the head. "No one's taking my grandbabies away."

CHAPTER NINETEEN

THE NEXT MORNING started early. Nana stood in the doorway. "Time to wake up, Riley. Today's a big day. We need to go shopping. Get the kitten up, time's a wasting."

After a quick breakfast, Nana took them on their morning walk around the farm, then they headed into town. Nana took them to a department store in Twin Falls, in a nice air-conditioned mall. They each got to pick one summer dress, two pairs of shorts, two tops, and a new pair of jeans. Riley couldn't remember ever having so many new clothes. Nana even bought them new underwear. Then she took them to the shoe section where they each got to choose a new pair of sandals and a pair of tennis shoes. Riley sat quietly in the car on the way home feeling totally overwhelmed. No one had ever spent so much money on them.

When they got home, Riley and Mia changed into their new shorts outfits and Nana made a big show of taking all their old clothes to the garbage can behind the house. She made them a quick lunch of sandwiches. Then she explained that they would be having company for supper and they needed to get busy. Nana assigned each of them chores: Mia dusted and Riley vacuumed. Nana killed and plucked two chickens, which made Riley feel a little sick, but the smell of frying chicken helped her get past it.

As she worked, Riley wondered who was coming. Would the sheriff and the social worker be back? Was Nana preparing their last supper together and buying them clothes because they were going to have to leave? At first, she was afraid to ask any questions, and then she didn't have time—Nana kept them running for hours.

The three of them were out in the garden picking tomatoes when Old Blue started screeching. Riley looked up to see a cloud of dust rolling up the lane at an alarming rate.

"Let's go, girls." Riley and Mia followed Nana to the front of the house. The dust cloud turned out to be Jack, the old man who had given them a ride only two days ago. Mia and Riley rushed out the gate and into his arms as he pulled himself out of the car. Nana shooed Old Blue away.

Jack laughed, patting the girls' hair. "Well, you two look a sight better than when I dropped you here. Life on the farm seems to agree with ya."

"I love it here!" exclaimed Mia, hopping through the gate and dashing to the bell, giving Jack a loud welcome clang.

Nana took them inside and got Jack settled at the table with a cup of coffee. Mia was telling Jack all about the kittens while Riley helped Nana bring the vegetables in from the garden. They had no sooner set down the baskets in the laundry room when Old Blue started shrieking again.

They all went outside as a blue minivan came up the driveway. Two boys about Mia's age tumbled out of the back seat and promptly ran off to climb on a tractor while a man and woman came around to meet them.

Riley was relieved to see it wasn't the sheriff or the social worker. The woman looked like a younger version of Nana. She was sturdily built and had the same halo of curls but her hair was dark brown.

Nana stood behind Riley and Mia, one hand on the shoulder of each. "Natalie and Chris, this is Riley." Nana took her hand off Riley's shoulder and touched the top of her head. "And this is Mia," she said, putting her hand on Mia's head.

"Girls, this is my daughter Natalie and her husband Chris."

Natalie smiled at them warmly and bent to shake their hands. Riley stared up into her smiling eyes. If this was Nana's daughter, that made her Daddy Blaine's sister and...Riley's aunt. She had an aunt and an uncle! That made the boys...

"Boys." Natalie's shout echoed Riley's thoughts. "Come meet your cousins."

The two dark-haired boys climbed slowly off the tractor and ran to their mother. One had curly hair like his mother and grandmother and one had straight hair like his dad.

"Riley and Mia," Natalie said, "This is your cousin, Hudson." She waved at the curly-haired boy. "And this is Lewis." She pointed to the straight-haired boy. "They're six."

"Are they twins?" asked Riley.

"We are," the boys said in unison.

"But you don't match," Mia said.

"We're not identical," Hudson said.

"Don't I even get a hug?" asked Nana. The boys bounded forward and smothered their nana in hugs and kisses.

Riley felt a stab of jealousy. She hadn't even thought about having to share her new nana with anyone except Mia.

"Mia," Nana said, "Would you like to take the boys down to meet the kittens?"

The three started to race away but their mother called the boys back. She bent down, taking an arm of each boy. "Kittens are very breakable," Natalie said in a serious voice. "You must hold them very gently...promise?"

The boys nodded solemnly and turned to follow Mia into the barn. Natalie turned to Chris. "I'll make sure," he said and followed the children into the barn.

"Come on, Riley," Nana said. "Let's help Natalie with her pies."

Natalie opened the back of the minivan and Riley saw four beautiful pies in towel-lined boxes. Nana handed her a box, then picked up one of her own, but before they could get through the gate Old Blue screeched again. A white SUV drove up the lane and Riley was introduced to more relatives.

She had another aunt and uncle and two precious little girls, one not even old enough to walk! Riley's head spun. How many relatives were coming? Did this mean her dad was coming, too? How many cousins did she have to share Nana with, anyway? Then Riley's stomach clenched—did her dad have any kids? She'd never thought about that. What if he had kids and didn't want her.

The little house was crowded with kids running in and out. Nana shouted at them to keep the screen door closed to keep the flies out. Riley caught her new relatives staring when they thought she wasn't looking. There was no sign of her father. Maybe he hadn't been able to get the cows up to their new pasture yet.

She found herself sitting on the floor of the living room playing with her little cousin, Bella, while freshly-baked bread smells filled the air, causing her stomach to rumble. The sun was going down and it was almost time for supper. She should be happy. She had always longed for a big family, and here they were. But she felt sad and...separate from all the people here. Riley's throat started to close and she blinked back tears. What was wrong with her?

Old Blue screeched and Riley jumped to her feet, running to the window to see a huge green pickup round the last turn up the driveway. Her heart skipped and she ran out on the porch. A short, round woman with long red hair was stepping out on the passenger side. A tall thin man in a cowboy hat came around the front of the truck and took the woman's hand.

Riley couldn't help herself. She was drawn down the steps like a moth to a flame. Mia came up behind her and took her hand. The rest of the family held back, gathering on the porch.

The man opened the gate, letting his wife through in front of him. The pair came toward the girls and stopped. The man bent down on one knee and slowly took off his hat.

Everything disappeared as Riley stared into his face. The man had a long thin face, blonde hair, a straight nose, and a very high forehead. The same kind of forehead that she had. Riley smiled shyly. He smiled back with the same shy smile.

The woman—Delly?—bent toward the girls. Her round face dimpled as she smiled. "Well, you are two of the prettiest girls I ever did see. Don't you think so, Blaine?"

The man swallowed hard and nodded, his eyes sparkling with what looked like tears. He turned to his wife. She nodded.

"We are mighty glad to meet you both," Delly said.

Riley's heart swelled. Was this it then? Had she actually found him?

The thin man...Blaine...her *father*...gave her another quiet smile. "Welcome home, little Riley. Welcome home."

About the Author

J ACCI LIVES WITH HER husband in Nevada's high desert. They spend their mornings hiking through the sagebrush with their big yellow dog, Rocky. Jacci loves chocolate, babies, and coffee with friends. She's worn many hats in her lifetime: therapist, school counselor, campus minister, and mom. Her favorite hats are her writer and grandmother hats, which come in wild colors and don't fit too tightly. In addition to sharing her stories about Riley and Mia, Jacci is the author of the Amazon best-selling young adult novel, *The Cage*, the first book in The Birthright series.

Made in the USA
Charleston, SC
29 October 2013